HEROES OF THE OGONI STRUGGLE

AND THE INVISIBLE VICTIMS

HEROES OF THE OGONI STRUGGLE

AND THE INVISIBLE VICTIMS

AUSTIN LEMEA

PRIMIX PUBLISHING
THE WRITE CHOICE

Primix Publishing
485c US Highway 1 South
Suite 100
Iselin, NJ 08830
www.primixpublishing.com
Phone: 1-800-538-5788

Published by Primix Publishing: 02/05/2025

ISBN: 979-8-89194-283-7(sc)
ISBN: 979-8-89194-444-2(hc)
ISBN: 979-8-89194-284-4(e)

Library of Congress Control Number: 2024916431

CONTENTS

Chapter 1.   The Ogoni People 1

Chapter 2.   Oil Discovery 3

Chapter 3.   The Environmental Degradation: 7

Chapter 4.   Ken Saro-Wiwa 9

Chapter 5.   MOSOP 11

Chapter 6.   The January 4, 1993, Protest 13

Chapter 7.   Politics 17

Chapter 8.   Election Boycott 21

Chapter 9.   The Murder at Gio-Khoo 25

Chapter 10. The Execution of the Ogoni Nine 33

Chapter 11. Reactions to the Ogoni Nine Executions 37

Chapter 12. January 4, 1996. Protest 41

Chapter 13. Federation of Ogoni Women Association
             (FOWA) 45

Chapter 14. Border Crossing. 49

Chapter 15. The Refugee Camp 55

Chapter 16. Nonu's Trip to Ghana 61

Chapter 17. Under the Mango Tree 71

Chapter 18. Resettlement 75

Chapter 19. The America's Problems. 83

Chapter 20. Nonu Relocated 101

Chapter 21. Deadly Encounter 111

Chapter 22. The Funerals 115

Chapter 23. Beneath the Guilt 119

Chapter 24. Dee Travels 125

Chapter 25. The Two Bonding Bodies 129

CHAPTER 1

THE OGONI PEOPLE

When the Great hero of all time Ken Saro-Wiwa stood on the stage at one of the elite school's playgrounds in Ogoni, microphone in his left hand, and raised his right hand to the sky and said "No to Shell," echoed by the 30,000 Ogoni people who had come out to protest against environmental degradation, economic strangulation, and a large-scale political marginalization on January 4, 1993, no one thought many heroes would emerge in Ogoniland. Like Kenule Beeson Saro-Wiwa, many had died. Many are alive. And most of them had been displaced due to intense persecution and death threats on their lives. But who are the Ogoni people, and where are they located in Nigeria?

The Ogoni are a minority ethnic group who live in the Western Niger Delta Region of southern Nigeria. They are perhaps the oldest settlers of the Eastern Niger Delta, living south of Igbo settlements, west of Ibibio communities, and inland from Obolo and Ijaw villages near the Atlantic coast.

According to oral tradition, the Ogoni people migrated from

ancient Ghana in West Africa to the Atlantic coast, then to the eastern Niger Delta region, where they merged with the Igbo and Ijaw populations. The name, "Ogoni," comes from the Ibani and the Ijaw word "Ogoni" which means STRANGERS.

Numbering about one million, the Indigenous people are blessed with alluvia soil and other natural mineral resources, including crude oil under their feet. Surrounded by water, the Ogoni people occupied themselves with subsistence farming and fishing. Their traditional diet includes cassava, yam, thick fresh and dried fish of several types and vegetables. The rich food combination not only provides nourishment but also serves as an economic resource, and cultural and spiritual identity. Their palm produce was the best in that part of the Niger. Their farm produce created a food surplus not only for them but for the entire Rivers State, giving them the nickname "Food Basket of Rivers State." However, Ogoniland agricultural production rapidly declined due to oil pollution and soil fertility issues. The people of Ogoni, once proud stewards of their lush and bountiful land, watched helplessly as their fields turned barren. The once vibrant green expanses, teeming with crops ready for harvest, now lay desolate and cracked under the relentless sun. Land degradation had set in.

CHAPTER 2

OIL DISCOVERY

Oil was discovered in Ogoniland in 1958. As my great grandpa puts it, "Beneath the mango trees, elders gathered, their eyes alight with visions of progress as oil workers and government agents stood before us and promised schools, hospitals, and paved roads. It was like a future painted in hues of prosperity." Grandpa concluded. "Then what happened after the promises?" I asked my grandpa and expected a response but I quickly interjected with another question. "Is that how the dirty-looking and empty hospital we went to the other day was built?" "Well, not sure. It was guessed at the time that Birabi built it. They never detailed how, but his name was synonymous with it." My Grandpa informed. "But what happened after the oil started flowing?" I asked again almost at once after my grandpa finished talking.

"Black gold flowed, but so did our worries. Would our rivers remain clean? Our forests untouched?" I couldn't understand Grandpa's response. I was young and still in elementary school. I never knew what was called poetry at the time. So, when Grandpa kept responding to me poetically, I kind of felt frustrated and agitative. At 89, Grandpa's voice was difficult to understand clearly. But he continued to narrate the ordeals that oil discovery brought to the land with his difficult-to-hear voice:

"Anger and Betrayal, it was." Grandpa went on "Our ancestral lands desecrated, we felt betrayed. The oil companies profited while we suffered. The land, once sacred, bore the scars— A map of greed etched upon its skin. Oilmen arrived, pockets lined with promises, yet beneath their boots, roots screamed in agony."

I was one of the curious kids around. I always carried a pocket dictionary in my book bag. So, once I heard the word agony, I excused Grandpa just to go and search for the meaning of the word in my half-turn pocket dictionary. When I returned, I asked Grandpa, "What did you say you were in pain and suffering for?" Grandpa chuckled and coughed out mucus, clearing his throat without giving me a specific answer. "But who is Birabi?" I asked, with my eyes fixated on Grandpa's "Nonu." Grandpa called out my name. "Yes, Grandpa," I responded. "Get me that picture frame on the wall." Grandpa said, pointing at a picture frame on the right side of the wall. Almost immediately, I jumped to my feet, walked by him, and grabbed the ancient-looking dusty picture frame. I barely saw the image in the frame nor recognized the face of who was in it due to the deterioration the picture had become. I handed it over to Grandpa. He wiped dust off the frame, Grandpa said: "This is Birabi. He was the first educated man Ogoni had when Shell came. He had all the documents concerning drilling agreements, but he died without any clear cause. He must have been poisoned." Grandpa said with raw emotion on his face. Pausing, he looked at the picture in his shaky hands, wiped the screen again with his bare right palm, and continued his lamentation.

"After Hon. Naakuu Timothy Paul Birabi died, everything turned apart. Fear and uncertainty set in. Drills pierced the earth, unearthing secrets. Oil spills filled the land and river while gas flares filled the air, burning the lungs of children. Hope and fear danced their age-old duet. The viable agricultural life of Ogoni disappeared. Then in the heart of Ogoniland, whispers rose." Grandpa suddenly stopped. After a few seconds and he wasn't saying anything, I asked him what the whispering was about. "You won't understand, Nonu," Grandpa said and turned his face to look at the picture in his hands again.

Yes, Grandpa was right. I wasn't going to understand. Only 12 years of age. I have not understood life in general nor that of the Ogoni people. However, I can recall vividly hearing my mother complaining of crops not doing good on her farmland and how hard it was becoming to buy fish in the market. I Understand that the scarcity of fish was due to oil spillage that had tainted the rivers, causing the rivers to murmur ancient warnings while the currents tainted by oily tears made the fish unable to leap silver-scaled and free. I remember seeing fishermen returning home and engaging in various forms of craftsmanship and artistic works. I remember seeing the traditional fishing, farming, and trading for livelihood fading and disappearing. I also remember witnessing the actual negative impacts of oil exploration and production in Ogoniland.

September 1992, I had just started High School after the death of my grandpa. My first week at school was supposed to be an exciting week, right? That was not the case. On one fateful afternoon, class in session, but a woman, escaping rape attack from men laying oil pipes across her farmland, rushed into the class, in which I was supposed to be having lessons. In panic mode, every member of the class including the teacher, who was giving lecture, jumped out through the opened windows. On the face of everyone, fear and shock dueled. No one knew what would come next. The woman, profusely sweating, half naked, sat on the classroom floor with legs spread out, her hands raised up, wailing:

"The hot sun has stolen my voice, echoing these fractured laments to silent trees and stained rivers. Their hands were as rough as their hearts, carving scars of shame into my soul, and the land, once lush and kind, now mirrors my pain - bruised, polluted, lifeless. How can I reclaim the dignity they tore away under the cold, merciless glare of the oil towers? My cries mingle with the suffocating ooze, each tear a drop of my lost essence, my stolen spirit. Who hears the wails of a woman eclipsed by greed, her agony buried in the shadow of a monstrous thirst?"

The woman had been raped while trying to block the oil workers from laying pipe over her crops. The following week, a female student was declared missing. The school was abruptly shot down. Students returned home to their parents. I had left the village and went to the city to inform my father of what was going on. I took a taxi and on the car radio, I heard the announcer mention a name that almost sounds familiar. "3:00pm on Sunday, Ken Saro-Wiwa would be our guest on Meet the Press." The announcement read. At the time, I never knew who Ken Saro-Wiwa was. For that reason, I had to keep that info in mind so I can listen in on the program when it would air.

CHAPTER 3

THE ENVIRONMENTAL DEGRADATION:

Since the Shell Petroleum Development Company discovered oil in Ogoniland, over one hundred oil wells were established, leading to serious environmental degradation. Thousands of oil spill incidents occurred, polluting land, rivers, and forests. Ogoni residents who depended on farming and fishing suffered direct impacts on their livelihoods. Besides the crops no longer yielding good produce, oil companies' heavy machinery would bulldoze crops already planted by the local farmers to create paths for their pipelines. This became a frequent occurrence without adequate compensation.

The other day, at about 4 pm Wednesday, the news of Shell's bulldozer damaging plants on people's farmland filtered into town. People whose farmlands are located around the area trooped down to witness it. I had to go with my mother to see things for myself. When we arrived, I could not believe what she was seeing. Everything green that was on the farm lay lifeless in a pile of rubble. Crying, my mother picked what she could lay her hands on to the front of

Shell's truck that was packed nearby and dropped them, piece by piece, lamenting as she did. Amid the golden hues of the sinking sun, I stood at the edge of her once-thriving farm and watched. Her voice broke into a heart-wrenching wail. The vibrant greens of her cassava and yam plants now lay scorched and lifeless, a cruel testament to the oil activities that had seeped into the fertile Ogoni soil overnight. Tear-streaked cheeks revealed her pain as she knelt, clutching the blackened remains of her hopes and dreams. "Ahhh! My God! What have they done to my land?" she cried, her voice echoing across the empty fields. The fruits of her labor, the sustenance of her family, drowned in a sea of crude devastation, leaving her spirit as broken as the charred remains beneath her fingers.

Health issues were widespread, and life expectancy in Ogoni dropped to 41 years, ten years lower than the national average. In the face of adversity, the Ogoni people stood together—MOSOP was born and the struggle for justice and environmental restoration began.

CHAPTER 4

KEN SARO-WIWA

Before the Ogoni Struggle, Ken Saro-Wiwa was a prolific Nigerian writer and television producer. Born on October 10, 1941, in Bori, the traditional headquarter of the Ogoni people, he excelled academically, eventually attending the University of Ibadan where he studied English. His early career saw him making significant contributions to Nigerian literature and media; he authored several novels, including "Sozaboy: A Novel in Rotten English," and produced a popular satirical television series, "Basi & Company," which critiqued Nigerian society with wit and humor. Saro-Wiwa also held various governmental positions, including the Regional Commissioner for Education in Rivers State. Despite his professional success, he increasingly became aware of the environmental degradation and social injustices faced by the Ogoni people due to the extensive oil extraction by multinational corporations. These injustices sowed the seeds of his later activism but before fully committing to the Ogoni Struggle, his life was characterized by a blend of literary achievement and social critique. On becoming a devoted environmentalist, Ken Saro-Wiwa registered Ogoni with the Unrepresented Nations and People's Organization (UNPO), of which he became Vice President,

CHAPTER 5

MOSOP

In 1990, Ogoni leaders, including environmental activist Ken Saro-Wiwa, founded the Movement for the Survival of the Ogoni People (MOSOP). MOSOP aimed to stop the exploitation of Ogoni by oil companies and the government. With the foundation of MOSOP, a declaration of the Ogoni Bill of Rights, which outlines the political demands of the Ogoni people, was made and submitted to the Nigerian government. In the OBR, Ogoni demanded an autonomous region where Ogoni may have its laws and the right to control a fair proportion of the resources available and allocate them as they so wish. MOSOP would be the key actor, under the leadership of Ken Saro-Wiwa, to propose these political demands to the government and the multinationals in the region. The movement has many wings such as the Federation of Ogoni Women (FOWA), National Youth Council of Ogoni People (NYCOP), National Union of Ogoni Students (NUOS), Ogoni Council of Churches (OCC), Council of Ogoni Traditional Rulers Association (COTRA), Ogoni Teachers Union (OTU), and Ogoni Students Union (OSU). The latter was formed for kids in high schools. There was the Traders Union, for those in the business sectors. The Ogoni movement was purely grassroots base. There was something for everyone.

In 1992, The Ogoni issued an ultimatum to Shell with five key demands. What followed almost immediately after was a series of peaceful mass protests reaching hundreds of thousands, the first of which would leave a lasting impression on Ogoni civil society. That was January 4th, 1993. This day would be the official Ogoni Day. MOSOP Steering Committee nominated Ken Saro-Wiwa to be the Ogoni Spokesperson.

CHAPTER 6

THE JANUARY 4, 1993, PROTEST

January 4th, 1993, was D-Day for the Ogoni people, old and young. It was the day to stage the first major protests for what had plagued them for decades. It was Ogoni Day, as it is popularly called. By 8 am, I had arrived at the Birabi Memorial Grammar School soccer field, the protest ground with bunch of leaves in my hands, like everyone else. As I arrived, more than 20,000 people were already there in upbeat spirits. It was all drumming and dancing. The air was electric with tension, the murmur of thousands of voices blending into a steady hum of anticipation and defiance made me hyper. Banners emblazoned with sharp, urgent messages waved high above the crowd, their colors stark against the dull gray sky. In any direction I turned, I saw pockets of people exchanging hopeful glances, sharing bottled water and makeshift snacks. The scent of smoke from a nearby bonfire mixed with the faint aroma of roasted street food, creating a strangely intoxicating atmosphere that felt both volatile and strangely unifying. Above all, the sign of solidarity was vividly clear. Then, more people continued to drop in. The most interesting part was my realization that almost everybody was anxious to see Ken Saro-Wiwa.

When he finally arrived, the air buzzed with anticipation as the crowd gathered at the edge of the street, eyes straining for the first glimmer of Ken's arrival. When his gleaming motorcade rounded the corner, a collective gasp rippled through the sea of onlookers. Cheers erupted, a cacophony of voices blending into a single, roaring wave of sound. Children hanging on trees just to catch a glimpse, adults stood on tiptoe, waving frantically, while the crowd broke into spontaneous applause, their faces lit with admiration and excitement. Ken's confident smile, half-hidden beneath his MOSOP face cap only intensified the crowd's exhilaration. As he slowed to a stop and dismounted, the cheering reached a fevered pitch, echoing through the bustling avenue and marking the moment with an indelible sense of triumph and unity. Ken Saro-Wiwa shook hands with distinguished guest sited under canopies, then climbed onto the stage, microphone in his left hand, and chanted: "No to Shell." The crowd repeated after him: "No to Shell." The chants rose and fell like powerful waves, each repetition more fervent than the last, as if the very ground beneath their feet demanded justice. Faces, flushed with determination, glistened with sweat even if it wasn't noon. When the chants faded, Ken acknowledged all the Kingdoms of Ogoni, then, delivered his speech:

Today is a great day for the Ogoni people. We are gathered here to commemorate our struggle, our resilience, and our collective determination to reclaim our rights and protect our environment. Ogoni Day is not just a date on the calendar; it is a symbol of our unity and our resolve to fight against oppression and exploitation. For years, our land has been ravaged by the insidious operations of multinational oil companies. Our rivers, once teeming with life, are now poisoned; our soil, once fertile and bountiful, is now barren and lifeless. Our people have borne the brunt of this ecological catastrophe, yet our cries have largely fallen on deaf ears. We must remind the Nigerian government and the world that our demands are rooted in justice and equity. We seek an end to the environmental devastation that has plagued our homeland. We demand fair compensation for the damage done to our livelihoods. We call for the restoration of our environment and the right to manage our resources in a sustainable and beneficial manner.

Our Movement for the Survival of the Ogoni People (MOSOP) was born out of a deep-seated need to address these grievances. Our non-violent struggle is aimed at achieving autonomy and ensuring that our people have a say in the use of our resources. We are committed to achieving these goals through peaceful means, despite the numerous challenges we face.

Our struggle is not in isolation. It is part of a broader fight for human rights and environmental justice across the Niger Delta and beyond. We stand in solidarity with all marginalized communities whose rights are trampled upon and whose environments are destroyed by powerful and unscrupulous entities.

On this Ogoni Day, I urge every one of you to remain steadfast in our cause. Let us draw strength from our shared heritage and our collective spirit. Let us continue to advocate for our rights with unwavering resolve, knowing that our struggle is just and that our voices, when united, can never be silenced. May we remain vigilant and courageous in the face of adversity. Together, we will forge a future where our children can live in harmony with their environment, free from the shadows of exploitation and oppression. Let this Ogoni Day be a reaffirmation of our commitment to justice, our dedication to peace, and our optimism for a brighter tomorrow.

As Ken's voice rose, resonating with conviction, I felt an unexpected lump form in my throat. Clutching the edge of my coat, I scanned the faces around me and saw the same blend of hope and determination mirrored in their eyes. The fervor in Ken's words seemed to echo the unspoken fears and dreams of every person present, and for a moment, the uncertainty of the future seemed to dissolve. I had never been particularly political, but standing there, surrounded by the buzzing energy of the crowd, I found myself nodding along, my heart beating in time with the rhythmic cadence of his speech. Tears welled up, not from sadness, but from a newfound sense of unity and purpose that Ken's words instilled in me and the sea of strangers beside me.

CHAPTER 7

POLITICS

The January 4th protest was a success. BBC, VOA, and some Nigerian news media carried the story, making it national and international news. As the Ogoni campaign to end environmental degradation and exploitation began to gain international popularity, Shell Oil could not rest on its oars as the company began to feel embarrassed. At home in Nigeria, the news swept through political corridors, and the lush green canopy of the Niger Delta seemed to echo with the calls for justice shaking the very foundations of the government's stronghold. In the grand halls of Abuja, the military head of State, Gen. Babangida convened an emergency session with his cabinet. The eyes of the nation were on them, and whispers of international intervention loomed like dark clouds over Aso Rock. Faced with mounting pressure, the administration had to navigate the volatile political landscape, balancing the demands for economic stability with the urgent cries for environmental justice. In the emergency session convened by Babangida, a Muslim man from the north, the Provisional Ruling Council promulgated the so-called "Civil Disturbance Decree" to crush the Ogoni environmental campaigns. Shell, whose operations had been disrupted, was becoming anxious about the unrest. The company was also aware the cries of the Ogoni people could no longer be ignored. And the only way to slow things down was to stop Ken Saro-Wiwa. Senators from the north who were mostly benefiting from oil sales were taking matters personal. Senator Malik, a politician and businessman with deep roots in oil business, paced his mahogany-furnished office, saying the protest might ignite a storm that could threaten to upend his oil business. "This nonsense has to stop." Senator Malik, a Muslim from the north where no oil is drilled and no environmental issues, declared. Not quite long after, Ogoni started feeling the brunt, starting from Ken himself, who suffered multiple arrests. With his movements restricted, his traveling passport was ceased. The military government, being the only beneficiary of oil revenues, swore to do whatever it takes to frustrate the Ogoni campaign. Using neighboring communities with the Ogoni was one way.

A few months after the mass demonstration on Jan. 4th, several Ogoni communities began to experience dangerous attacks from their neighbors with whom they had lived in peace before the campaign. It was around 4am and residents of Kpeah community were still sleeping. But the early morning silence was shattered by the wailing of men, women, and children as the government sponsored bandits descended upon the small village. People stumbled out of their homes, eyes wide with fear, clutching whatever possessions they could carry. Mothers clung to their crying children, trying to shield them from danger. Elderly men, their faces etched with lines of worry, stood helplessly as invaders tore through their belongings. The air was thick with the acrid smell of smoke as fires broke out, and the once peaceful village was engulfed in a haze of panic and despair. Bullets pierced through human souls, causing lifeless bodies to litter the ground. Cries for mercy mingled with the authoritative shouts of the troops, creating a cacophony of anguish that echoed off the surrounding hills. In that moment, their lives were irrevocably altered, their futures consumed by the uncertainty and fear that the raid had brought upon them. Life was never the same anymore. Reports of similar attacks came in from several communities around the coastal line throughout Ogoniland. Hundreds of people died in some of the attacks. Some were burnt to death.

Meanwhile, serious division had surfaced on the home front. Some of the prominent Ogoni chiefs and politicians had fallen away from Ken Saro-Wiwa and MOSOP. They had gone to the press to denounce MOSOP and Ken Saro-Wiwa. The balkanization had stemmed from an idea MOSOP was mulling. Movement for the Survival of the Ogoni People (MOSOP) wanted to boycott the 1993 presidential election to show anger for unfair treatment Ogoni had suffered. But that did not sit well with Ogoni politicians who had situated themselves with various political parties in the country, promising to deliver Ogoni votes to them. To these politicians, an election boycott was a line not to be crossed, irrespective of the consequences.

CHAPTER 8

ELECTION BOYCOTT

The sun had barely risen when Ogoni youths, heeding the call of Ken Saro-Wiwa and MOSOP, began assembling at strategic locations across Ogoniland. There was an air of resolute determination as they prepared to enforce the boycott of the June 12, 1993, Presidential election. Banners and placards proclaiming, "Our Land, Our Rights" and "No Vote, No Betrayal" were held high. The streets were alive with chants calling for justice and recognition of their plight. At polling stations, Ogoni youths had formed human barricades. They stood firm, preventing entry and calmly explaining their stance to any who approached. Some voters, understanding the gravity of the situation, turned back in solidarity. Those more determined to vote found themselves in heated dialogues with the youths, often culminating in the decision to leave rather than engage in conflict.

Politicians sent emissaries to negotiate, offering promises of development, aid, and political recognition. The youths listened but remained unmoved. Their leaders had made it clear—no promises could be trusted from those who had repeatedly betrayed their cause.

As news spread about the widespread boycott, tension reached a boiling point. Authorities, attempting to salvage the election, dispatched security forces to escort voters and protect polling stations. The presence of armed personnel only fueled the resolve of Ogoni youths. Skirmishes broke out at several locations, but the youths' sheer numbers and determination made it clear that any attempt to forcefully conduct the elections would only lead to chaos.

By midday, it was apparent that the boycott was overwhelmingly successful. Polling stations in Ogoniland were largely deserted. Politicians, realizing that coercion would not yield the desired results, began to withdraw, directing their focus to areas with less resistance. Reports of the boycott began hitting national and international news, painting a vivid picture of a community's struggle for justice and autonomy.

As the day drew to a close, the streets of Ogoniland were filled with a mix of exhaustion and triumph. The youths had not only halted the election but had also sent a powerful message. Their voices, echoing the hopes and demands of an entire community, could not be silenced. Though the struggle for recognition and justice was far from over, the success of the boycott was a testament to their unity and unyielding spirit.

The politics in Ogoniland has deeply tainted the integrity of its leaders, transforming once-respected figures into pawns of self-interest and corruption. Driven by a mixture of external pressures and internal rivalries, these leaders have often prioritized personal gain over the welfare of their communities, succumbing to the allure of political patronage. This corrosive influence has led to compromised decisions that neglect essential developmental projects and environmental protections crucial for the Ogoni people. Consequently, the repercussions of such political manipulation have not only eroded public trust but have also entrenched socioeconomic disparities, leaving the Ogoni populace disenchanted and disillusioned with their leadership. While Ken was far away in London, the youth arm of MOSOP followed through the decision not to participate in the June 12th, 1993, presidential election.

A day prior to the election, youths in all villages and towns of Ogoni made it clear to all that Ken said there should be no election in Ogoniland. And that any who attempted to do otherwise would have him/herself to blame. So, the day came. In the early morning mist of June 12, the usually bustling streets of Ogoniland were eerily silent. The vibrant markets and lively communal spaces stood empty, only the youths enforcing the no election order were seen at polling locations, a stark testament to the unity and resolve of the Ogoni people. Ken Saro-Wiwa's call for a boycott of the presidential election had resonated deeply, a powerful statement against the systemic exploitation and neglect by the Nigerian government. As the rest of the country engaged in the electoral process, Ogoni towns and villages became symbols of peaceful protest. The absence of voting lines and campaign posters underscored a community's collective demand for justice, environmental stewardship, and genuine autonomy. The boycott wasn't just an act of defiance; it was a profound expression of marginalized people's cry for recognition and respect. However, this singular act led to the resignations of other MOSOP leaders, particularly the 'Ogoni Four. The politicians, on their part, were taken aback by the sheer scale of the mobilization. Just days before, they were confident that the elections would proceed without a hitch. Now, facing a united front of determined youths, they quickly convened in makeshift offices to devise new strategies. Time was not on their side as voting hours approached and plans to ensure voter turnout bordered on desperation.

The Ogoni community, like many ethnic groups, is not monolithic. There were existing local rivalries and divisions that influenced political alliances and oppositions. These intra-communal dynamics did translate into opposition to Saro-Wiwa. More so was his idea to boycott the election. Opposing Ogoni leaders were always on radio, Television, new magazines and newspapers, dishing and discrediting Ken Saro-Wiwa, labelling him 'Authoritarian.' The murmurs of agreement grew louder, echoing the sentiment that while Saro-Wiwa's passion was undeniable, his tactics were increasingly seen as a double-edge sword, risking the very survival of the Ogoni people.

CHAPTER 9

THE MURDER AT
GIO-KHOO

After the election boycott, the stage was set for rivalry, and tension built between other Ogoni leaders and Ken Saro-Wiwa. Both external and internal opposition towards Ken and MOSOP was rapidly rising high. Opposing Ogoni leaders were always on radio, Television, new magazines and newspapers, dissing and discrediting Ken Saro-Wiwa, labelling him 'Authoritarian.' In the days following the election boycott, palpable tension hung over Ogoniland. At a hastily convened meeting in a dimly lit community hall, a group of Ogoni leaders who had opposed Ken Saro-Wiwa's call for a boycott voiced their frustrations. Chief Nwafor, a respected elder with ties to the State government rose to speak, his voice heavy with anger.

"While I understand the grievances of our people, this boycott has only deepened our isolation," he began, his eyes scanning the room filled with anxious faces. "We have now missed an opportunity to influence the national dialogue and advocate for our rights from within the system. The government will see this as a rejection of engagement, and I fear it will bring harsher reprisals upon our community." Another leader, Madam Vikus, the only female figure in the opposing group, also voiced her concern. "Ken's intentions are noble, but his methods are dividing us. We need a strategy that balances protest with negotiation. By boycotting, we've handed our adversaries a reason to dismiss our struggle as radical and uncooperative." Of course, harsher reprisals came to Ogoni communities.

What happened to Ken Saro-Wiwa, and the entire Ogoni communities can be adequately compared to what happened in Kalavryta, Greece, during World War II of 1943. Although they differ significantly in context and scope, both have historical context and are tragic events rooted in acts of retaliation and suppression. Kalavryta events occurred during World War II. Perpetrators, German troops. Victims were Primarily the male population of Kalavryta. Reason, Retaliation for Greek resistance activities. The nature of the event was a mass execution of civilians (mainly men) and extensive destruction of the town that was left in devastation with severe loss of life among the male population. The historical context of the Ogoni case is that it occurred in the early 1990s, and was in Ogoniland, Nigeria, Africa. The perpetrators were Nigerian government forces. The victims were the Ogoni ethnic group. The reason was eerily similar. Suppression of resistance against environmental degradation and political activism. The nature of the event was the systematic killing, displacement, and imprisonment of the Ogoni people. The immediate outcome was large-scale human rights abuses, environmental destruction, and long-term suffering for the Ogoni community.

So, in Comparison, both events involve state or occupying forces retaliating against perceived resistance or dissent. In Kalavryta, the retaliation was against a specific resistance movement during an occupation in WWII, involving the execution of males and destruction in a single town. The Ogoni ethnic cleansing involved a broader, prolonged campaign of suppression targeting an entire ethnic group due to their environmental activism and opposition to governmental policies. Both led to significant loss of life and long-lasting impacts on the communities involved. However, the scale and methods differ, with Kalavryta being a focused, short-term atrocity, while the Ogoni case involved systematic oppression over a prolonged period. These events underline the destructive impacts of retaliatory violence and the suppression of dissent by authoritative powers.

Ken Saro-Wiwa returned to Ogoni and started to campaign for votes to represent Ogoni at the National Constitutional Conference that the federal government had scheduled to hold sometime in July of 1994. On June 23, Ken took his campaign tour to U-Town, and was to visit Gio-Khoo the next day, where he would address the youths. On June 24 when Ken was to enter Giokhoo as scheduled, he was blocked from entering that community by Nigerian soldiers, who turned him away. Some Ogoni leaders, who had deepened their hands in politics and were still angry about the 1993 presidential election boycott, were said to be holding meetings there at the time and they had ordered the soldiers to turn Ken away. What Ken Saro-Wiwa was doing was different from the traditional politics. He was informing the youths why it's important that he, Ken, represents Ogoni at the National Constitutional Conference. Ken wasn't campaigning to be voted into any electoral office. The youths wanted someone they trusted at the constitutional conference and not someone who would go and say something different. But the politicians misconstrued it. Frustrated, the youths of that community felt betrayed by their leaders for aligning with government and corporate interests that were at odds with Ogoni's stance against environmental degradation and exploitation for immediate benefits and political positions that could compromise the broader goals of environmental justice and self-determination championed by Saro-Wiwa. This clash of strategies created an atmosphere of mistrust and opposition, complicating the unified front needed for effective advocacy and resistance against external pressures. The youths did not like it. Before the opposing leaders' meeting could end, the youths stumped the venue. In the end, four leaders were mobbed, and they died in the process. Ken Saro-Wiwa was summarily arrested. Other MOSOP leaders were also rounded up and put in prison without any credible investigations. The clash between the old and the young, the powerful and the powerless, played out against a backdrop of a nation in flux, reflecting the raw and unyielding struggle for a better future. Arrested alongside Ken Saro-Wiwa were Saturday Dobee, Nordu Eawo, Daniel Gbooko, Paul Levera, Felix Nuate, Baribor Bera, Barinem Kiobel, and John Kpuinen.

Saro-Wiwa, alongside his comrades in the Movement for the Survival of the Ogoni People (MOSOP), became the faces of defiance, representing the collective anger and hope of a silenced populace. Yet, behind the prominent figures of this struggle, there lived the unseen, the unsung—those who toiled and suffered in obscurity. EbaBari, a young mother, watched helplessly as her children fell sick from polluted water. Her pleas for clean water went unheard, drowned out by the cacophony of industrial drills. Kinanee, a fisherman whose nets once brimmed with fish, now tossed them in vain into empty, tainted waters, his livelihood and dignity eroded by the same hands that built oil rigs on his ancestral grounds.

These invisible victims bore the brunt of the conflict. Their voices, though soft and often unheard, formed the true chorus of the Ogoni struggle. Every inhalation of toxic air, every barren harvest, every funeral for a child who drank from a poisoned well, added to the silent screams that fueled the movement. Faith, powered by ancestral lineage and an unbreakable bond to the land, kept their spirits alive. Women, like Mama Boonea, gathered in secret, sharing whispered prayers and rebellious songs, clothing their pain in traditions that predated the oil companies. Their resilience, though quiet, wove the fabric of resistance, stitching together the visible heroes with their unseen kin, sometimes shot at or killed during protest.

As the world watched, captivated by the eloquence of leaders like Saro-Wiwa, it was the unrecorded endurance of the everyday Ogoni that sustained the struggle. They were the invisible victims, the backbone of a fight that demanded not just justice, but recognition of their humanity. The Ogoni struggle is not merely a chapter in environmental activism but a testament to the indefatigable spirit of a people who refused to be erased. It is in remembering both the heroes and the invisible victims that we truly honor the legacy of Ogoniland. For it was through their collective sacrifice, seen and unseen, heard and unheard, that a flicker of hope was kindled in a world otherwise oblivious to their plight. For this reason, the arrest of the Nine did not end the military clampdown on Ogoni communities. While the Nine were facing trumped-up charges and sham trials, Ogoni communities were still boiling. Some members of the opposing group capitalized on military presence in Ogoni to unleash vendetta on those they deemed enemies. The incident in Uegwere town on June 6, 1994, serves as a testament.

In that town lives a high-ranking politician who will not want to hear anything about MOSOP or Ken Saro-Wiwa and will go to any length to deal with any supporters of the struggle. At the time of crisis in Ogoni, this politician was awarded a low-level contract by the government to clear off bushes at an oil well site in his community. What J.S. Sahga did with the money paid to him from the contract, was horrible. Sagha used the money to oppress those not loyal to him in his community. Worst still, Sagha went the extra mile by organizing thugs with the supervision of the military to murder a young man he's been targeting for a long time in his community.

June 6th, 1994, in the sleepy town of Uegwere, the dawn broke quietly, casting a soft golden hue over the rain-soaked land and ancient homes. The birds would have begun their morning chorus if not for the overnight rain. But despite the wetness, the community woke up to a glow of huge fire and smoke shooting up to the sky. Loud bomb-like sounds shattered the calm, drawing residents from their beds in confusion and fear. The work of Sagha, known for his ardent disagreement with MOSOP and supporters like Sorko Gbinee, a well-known MOSOP supporter, was visible. Sorko had been a local hero due to his strong involvement in the Ogoni struggle. He had a wife but no kids and was the firstborn of his mother. His father died mysteriously years back, and he was the only hope of the family. But that horrible morning, his dead body lay in a pile of charred rubles of roof that had crumbled down on his lifeless body. The dead body had no gunshot, no fire burns, just a naked body lay helplessly in the ash. As I and some friends arrived at the scene, our faces turned pale with shock and horror. Joy, Sorko's wife, collapsed to her knees, her wails echoing through the early morning air. The quiet town was suddenly alive with raw emotion—grief, anger, and disbelief swirling together in a chaotic blend. Family members, and friends, clutched one another, and tears streamed down our faces as we tried to make sense of the scene before us. Uegwere was never the same. The bond of trust between the people and leaders lay shattered, replaced by deep-seated mistrust and sorrow. Sorko was just one of the invisible victims of the struggle.

CHAPTER 10

THE EXECUTION OF
THE OGONI NINE

Under Major-General Sani Abacha, a military tribunal was constituted to try the Nine. The trial was widely discredited as it lacked fair legal procedures and was aimed at silencing protests against the oil company's bad practices. Despite international outcry and appeals for clemency, the Ogoni nine were executed by hanging on November 10, 1995. Before they died, something happened.

In the dim light of dawn, Ken Saro-Wiwa stood resolute, his heart a steady drumbeat against the chaos of his mind. The air was thick with the scent of rain-soaked earth, a poignant reminder of the Ogoniland he so dearly loved. Around him, his fellow activists, bound by chains but unbroken in spirit, shared silent glances of solidarity. As the guards led them to the gallows, a hush fell over the prison yard. Ken thought of the Ogoni people, their vibrant laughter, and their unyielding strength. He thought of the rivers, once teeming with life, now choked by oil. He thought of the future generations, for whom he hoped his sacrifice would not be in vain.

With each step, memories flickered like fireflies in the twilight of his mind—protests, speeches, moments of despair, and flashes of triumph. In the distance, a bird sang, its melody piercing the somber silence, a defiant cry of freedom that soared above the walls. Ken turned to his comrades, their eyes alight with a fire that no noose could extinguish. "We are the custodians of the earth," he whispered, his voice steady.

"Our struggle is a testament, not of defeat, but of our undying hope," Ken spoke the content of his mind. As they stood together, the Ogoni Nine faced their fate not as victims, but as heroes whose legacy would echo through the ages, a beacon of courage and an unending call to justice.

The guard attempted to hang the Nine, but each attempt was a failure. The machine would malfunction, signaling the unjust death they were about to face. Then, Ken invoked the spirit of Ogoni to let them die. "The world will hear our story," Ken vowed, his words a silent promise to the wind. "And though we fall today, the Ogoni struggle will live on, until the sun rises on a new day of freedom. Lord, take my soul, and let the struggle continue." Ken evoked. With that, they all stepped forward, their heads held high, leaving behind a silence that spoke louder than words ever could. The Nine died. And their lifeless bodies were dragged into a tipper (truck) and thrown into a single grave, their bodies mutilated further by the cruel pouring of raw acid, meant to speed up their decay.

This was not just an act of killing but a perverse mockery of life, a desecration of the very essence of humanity. It left a wound in the hearts of their loved ones, a wound that would never heal. The Ogoni people, who had braved persecution and fought relentlessly for their rights, felt an unspeakable pain. Mothers, fathers, wives, and children crumbled under the weight of their loss. The absence of justice, the cold cruelty of the punishment, and the utter disregard for human dignity were too much to bear. It was more than just a loss; it shattered their spirit, leaving them grappling with a void that words could never fill.

As days turned into nights, and nights into days, the memory of the Ogoni 9 lingered like a haunting ghost. Their sacrifices reverberated through the hearts of many, a stark reminder of the price of truth and justice in a world governed by corruption and greed. They were more than just victims; they were martyrs, and their unjust deaths became the rallying cry for justice and change. The sadness blanketing the Ogoni was palpable. It was a collective mourning, an emotional and spiritual destruction that no passage of time could repair. They were forced to carry on, their resilience and unity the only shields against the overpowering grief and the painful echo of their loved ones' cries for justice. In remembering the Ogoni 9, we honor not just their struggle but their unyielding spirit. They live on in the fight for human rights, in the unwavering demand for justice, and in every heart that dares to dream of a better, fairer world. They may have been reduced to bones and ashes, but their legacy is indestructible, etched into the fabric of our shared history, a beacon of courage amidst a sea of darkness.

They became the Heroes of the Ogoni Struggle.

The story of the Ogoni Nine is a poignant reminder of the cost of activism in the face of oppression and environmental exploitation. Their legacy lives on in the ongoing efforts to achieve justice and reparations for the Ogoni people and to hold accountable those responsible for environmental and human rights abuses in the Niger Delta.

CHAPTER 11

REACTIONS TO THE OGONI NINE EXECUTIONS

The atmosphere in Ogoniland after the deaths of the Ogoni Nine was of profound grief, outrage, and a heightened sense of injustice. The execution of these activists not only deepened the sorrow within the community but also galvanized the Ogoni people and others around the world to continue the fight for environmental justice and human rights. The community mourned the loss of their leaders and loved ones, who had become the symbols of resistance against exploitation and environmental degradation. There was widespread anger against the Nigerian government and Shell for their roles in the executions. This anger, however, was accompanied by a resilient determination to continue the struggle for which the Ogoni Nine had fought and died. On the international front, the execution sparked an international outcry and led to Nigeria's suspension from the Commonwealth of Nations. The global community rallied in support of the Ogoni cause, bringing further attention to the plight of the region.

A memorial event was held in honor of the Ogoni Nine the following day. That evening, the air was heavy with the scent of tropical rain, mingling with the somber tones of traditional Ogoni songs. Amidst fierce-looking soldiers with guns drawn, the community gathered, a sea of faces marked by the passage of time and the weight of shared history, ignored the soldiers' presence. In the heart of Ogoniland, under the shade of the ancient iroko trees, stands a simple stage adorned with nine chairs, each bearing the name of one of the fallen heroes. Elders and youths alike wear black armbands, a silent testament to their grief and unyielding resolve. Pictures of the Ogoni Nine are displayed prominently, their eyes gazing out at the crowd, a reminder of the price paid for daring to dream of justice. As the ceremony begins, a hush falls over the assembly. One by one, representatives from various communities step forward to pay tribute. They spoke of the courage and sacrifice of the Nine, and of the battles fought and the victories yet to come. Their words, punctuated by the soft thud of drums, were accompanied by intermittent sobs of those who remember. A moment of silence was observed. The quiet, so profound, it seemed to carry the whispers of the past, the hopes for the future. Candles were lit. Their flames flickering against the encroaching dusk, showed the symbols of hope in the face of darkness. Youths performed a poignant drama, reenacting the events that led to the tragic executions, while dancers moved to the rhythms of resistance, their bodies telling the story of a people's enduring spirit.

As the event neared its end, the names of the Nine were called out and the crowd responded, "Present!" affirming that though they are gone, they are not forgotten. The ceremony ended with a call to action, a renewed commitment to the struggle for which the

Ogoni Nine laid down their lives. The event ended with a solemn reverence, a poignant moment that captured the collective heartache of the community. An elderly woman, her face etched with the wisdom and sorrow of years, stepped forward to lay a wreath at the foot of the stage. Her hands, trembling with age and emotion, gently placed the flowers down as a tribute to the fallen heroes. The crowd watched in respectful silence, but as she turned to face the assembly, something shifted. The woman's stoic composure crumbled, and a single, heart-wrenching sob escaped her lips. It was a sound that resonated deeply, stirring a wave of empathy that rippled through the onlookers. Tears streamed down her cheeks, unbidden and unchecked, as she whispered the name of her son—one of the Ogoni Nine. Her voice, barely audible, carried the weight of a mother's love and loss. It's a personal grief, yet it echoed the collective mourning of all who had suffered. In this unexpected moment of vulnerability, the community's resolve was renewed. They gathered around her, offering support through gentle touches and shared tears. The woman's breakdown became a cathartic release, a symbol of the pain they all carry, and a reminder of why they continue to stand together in the face of adversity. This moment, raw and unguarded, serves as a powerful testament to the enduring impact of the Ogoni Nine. It's a reminder that behind the names and the cause are individual stories of love, loss, and the unbreakable bond of the community.

Amidst the crowd, a young girl named Nimi stood, her eyes fixed on the elderly woman's display of raw emotion. Nimi, in her early twenties, feels a profound connection to the pain and passion that fuels the movement, as she watches the elderly woman weep openly. The tears are not just of sorrow, but of resilience; they are a testament to the human spirit's capacity to endure and hope against all odds. At this moment, Nimi realizes that the struggle isn't just about political statements or environmental activism—it's deeply personal, woven into the very fabric of her community's identity. The sight of the community rallying around the grieving mother, their shared strength in the face of such palpable loss, ignites something within Nimi. She feels a renewed sense of purpose and a deep responsibility to carry forward the torch passed down by the Ogoni Nine. It's as if their spirits are there with her, whispering words of encouragement and solidarity. Nimi leaves the memorial with a quiet determination etched into her features. She understands that the journey ahead is fraught with challenges, but she's ready to face them head-on. Inspired by the collective show of strength, she vows to honor the memory of the Ogoni Nine through her actions and to be a voice for those who can no longer speak. This moment of shared grief and unity becomes a turning point for Nimi. She draws strength from the past, stands firmly in the present, and looks toward the future with unwavering resolve. Her path is clear, and she steps forward with the legacy of the Ogoni Nine lighting the way. But that was just the beginning of Nimi.

CHAPTER 12

JANUARY 4, 1996.
PROTEST

Determined and hardworking, Nimi Ngei was one of the main organizers of Jan. Fourth Protest of nineteen ninety-six. Nimi, at just 23 years old, worked tirelessly alongside other determined young women both from Ogoni and outside Ogoni to orchestrate the event that took place on January 4, 1996, following the tragic execution of the Ogoni Nine. The small, dimly lit room buzzed with activity as they sketched out plans on a massive chalkboard, outlining routes and safety procedures. The smell of freshly brewed coffee mingled with the scent of ink from hastily printed flyers. Nimi's eyes were fixed on the growing list of volunteers; each name was a beacon of hope in the midst of grief. They whispered fervent words of resilience and justice, their voices blending with the hum of the outdated fax machine churning out messages to activist groups across the state. Despite the palpable tension, a sense of unity and purpose filled the air, binding them together in their fight for justice.

On the day of protest, humid air hung thick with tension as a sea of determined faces reflecting collective grief and fury gathered to celebrate Ogoni Day in the oil city of Port Harcourt, Rivers State. The recent execution of the Ogoni Nine, including the charismatic activist Ken Saro-Wiwa, had ignited a fierce resolve among youths, and students from various institutions in the state, mothers with children, men, young and old. The crowd swelled, their chants echoing through the dense city, a chorus of defiance against the oppressive regime. Banners waved high, emblazoned with cries for justice and freedom, and the images of the fallen leaders. Suddenly, the crackle of gunfire shattered the charged atmosphere, sending shockwaves through the rally. Soldiers, their faces hidden behind cold, impassive masks, began firing sporadically into the air, the deafening sounds mingling with the screams and cries of the panicked crowd. Mothers clutched their children, dragging them to the ground, while men formed protective circles around the elderly and wounded. The soldiers advanced, their rifles raised, eyes scanning the mass of bodies for any sign of resistance. Smoke grenades were hurled, filling the air with acrid clouds that stung the eyes and choked the lungs. The crowd dispersed in chaotic waves, some fleeing into the surrounding trees. With my heart pounding hard, I ran in a different direction, stumbling over a pile of rocks. I was able to help myself up.

About to continue, I heard a voice calling my name, "Nonu, Nonu, please help!" I turned, a hand waving in the smoke grenade-filled air. It was Nimi. She had fallen into a muddy gutter and was not able to get out. "Come on, hold my hand," I said as I stretched out my right hand to render help. "Mhhh." Holding tightly onto my hand, Nimi screamed as she struggled to get out. "Oh my God, you'd never forgive these people, Huh, Huh," Nimi breathed heavily as she made it out. We both ran away but she went in a different direction. Still running, my phone suddenly vibrated, and stopped to answer it. It was my brother calling from Bori, Ogoni.

In the Ogoni mainland, the story was more deadly. My brother called me and said do not come home yet. "The atmosphere is tense." "What happened?" I asked like I was a stranger. "We had just gathered to celebrate Jan. 4th, when the soldiers arrived and started shooting and advancing into the crowd. Ndorbu Thompson, Lucky Gbarabe, and two other guys had been shot to death." My brother said in a panicked voice. A hush fell on me, I couldn't say a word anymore. Contorted with anger, I could not move. I stood under a tree for over 30 minutes hoping to hear any sound of gunfire. When the dust appeared to settle, I returned to the rally ground. The once vibrant rally ground lay in ruins. Torn banners fluttered like ghosts, and the echoes of gunfire slowly faded into an eerie silence. The soldiers stood victorious, their presence a stark reminder of the regime's iron grip. Yet amidst the chaos and carnage, a quiet resolve took root in the hearts of survivors. The spirit of the Ogoni Nine lived on, fueling a fire that no amount of oppression could extinguish.

CHAPTER 13

FEDERATION OF OGONI WOMEN ASSOCIATION (FOWA)

The Federation of Ogoni Women Association (FOWA) played a significant role in the Ogoni environmental struggle. They were actively involved in protests, advocacy, and community organizing efforts to address the environmental degradation caused by oil exploration and exploitation in the region. Women in Ogoni communities were at the forefront of resistance movements, raising awareness about the adverse effects of oil spills, pollution, and deforestation on their livelihoods, health, and environment. They organized rallies, demonstrations, and sit-ins, and often used traditional forms of protest, such as singing, dancing, and symbolic gestures, to amplify their voices and demand justice from the Nigerian government and multinational oil corporations.

Additionally, women provided crucial support networks within their communities, offering care, sustenance, and solidarity to fellow activists, and ensuring the continuity and resilience of the environmental struggle across generations. From the inception of MOSOP to the time the government used Ogoni neighbors to attack Ogoni communities to the execution of the Ogoni Nine, Ogoni women had been there holding prayer sessions or strategizing sessions. Before the soldiers secured the rally ground on Jan. 4, 1996, Madam Turreh, dressed in the traditional MOSOP attire, a face cap with the inscription "MOSOP" boldly written across the forehead, climbed the stage and spoke to her fellow Ogoni women's home and abroad.

"Great Ogoni Women!" "Great!" The crowd responded. "As the rivers weep and the land mourns, we rise united, sisters in the struggle, guardians of our homes, our voices, like the winds that sweep across our land, will not be silenced until justice flows like the clean waters of our ancestors." She continued. "From the depths of our hearts to the heights of the sky, we demand accountability for the destruction wrought upon our land. Let our footsteps echo the resilience of our foremothers as we march forward, daughters of the soil, defenders of our future. In the circle of our sisterhood, we find strength, wisdom, and the power to heal our wounded earth." A loud applause ensued amidst drum beats and clapping.

In one of their prayer sessions, a woman popularly known and called "Mama Bori" offered a prayer that touched souls. That morning, it was a fasting and praying session for the struggle. When it was her turn to pray, Mama Bori got up and shouted on top of her lungs, "Great Ogoni women!" "Great!" The congregation echoed. "Halleluiah!" "A-m-e-n…" They echoed, drawing on it for seconds like heaven would come down. Mama Bori continued. "O Great Mother Earth, hear our cries as we gather beneath your weary skies, grant us the strength to heal wounds and restore your beauty." She paused. Then, she fired on.

"Sovereign Spirit of the Delta, guide our hands and hearts as we stand as stewards of this sacred land, protect us as we strive for justice and harmony." She paused and watched the congregation nodding their heads in affirmation. Then continued: "May our prayers rise like incenses, reaching the heavens, invoking the wisdom of our ancestors to guide us in our quest for environmental liberation." "Yes!" A few shouted from the crowd. "Grant us courage to confront the darkness that plagues our land and may light of truth illuminate our path towards a future of abundance and peace." "Amen!" Echoed the crowd. "In the silence of our souls, we find communion with the spirits of the earth, listening to their whispers of hope and resilience, as we gather in solidarity and determination."

From rape by oil workers, and that of the internal military troops invading Ogoni communities, women faced challenges and risks within the struggle. The barriers they encountered were countless. Stemming from social expectations, gender-based violence, and the threat of reprisals from authorities and corporations, women made a lot of sacrifices for the greater good of the struggle. The solidarity and sisterhood that existed among women throughout the trial time were prevalent. They supported each other emotionally, spiritually, and practically, forming tight-knit bonds that sustained them through difficult times. These relationships served as a source of strength and resilience in the face of adversity. Their unwavering commitment to seeking justice inspired future generations to continue the fight for a more just and sustainable world. It's this commitment that inspired Nimi to stand out during the memorial for the Ogoni Nine and that of Jan. 4th, 1996. Nimi's inspiration put her on the military radar and made her a target for arrest, but she escaped to the refugee camp in the Benin Republic just like many other young activists. I was one of them.

CHAPTER 14

BORDER CROSSING

As the tension ran high, information reaching me had it that my name had been listed for arrest. I had no option but to vacate the area. I traveled through the night to Lagos with just one pair of shirts, one pair of long pants, and open-toe sandal shoes. A few weeks later, I got a delivery job with some Indians in the Victoria Island area of Lagos. Lucky for me the job came with accommodation. I had to live in the same compound with an ambassador from Zimbabwe, where my boss lived at the time. The security guard was a man from Liberia while the cook was from Benn Republic. I was the only Nigerian among them. Now and then, someone would interview me to know if I was really from Ogoni. And when I said yes, more questions would follow. I was becoming uncomfortable that I had to tell the Liberian man to show me the way to the American Embassy, that I was mulling the idea of leaving the country. "No, no, you cannot seek asylum while still living in your country. You must go to Ghana before you can seek asylum. That is what I did." Liberian man said. "But I do not have a passport. How would I get to Ghana." I said to Mr. Sam, as we used to call him. Mr. Sam was in his late 40s with some wisdom. The next day, the ambassador's daughter came to me and said that she heard I was looking to leave the country, "it's that true?" She asked kindly like she had interest. "Sure, sure, if that would be possible," I replied. "But you sure you're from Ogoni, Ken Saro-Wiwa's place?" "Yes, I am," I replied, taking a critical look at her just to know why she asked. On February 27, Sam asked if I was still willing to leave the country. I said yes to him. "Samuel, the cook is from Benin, and he would be traveling home to see his wife who had just given birth to a newborn baby. You can go with him. He will help you cross the border into Benin." Sam dropped the info. Instantly, my head spun. I took a long look at Sam, reading his mind to be sure he was telling the truth. I didn't have any money on me at the time. I don't know how am going to get to Benin. "Okay! Let me talk to my boss when he comes home." I said in response.

The following day, Mildred, the ambassador's daughter, gave me some money to buy some food and some clothes. I was elated to the point that my hands started shaking when I'm taking the money from her. On February 29, my boss came home in the evening. I walked to him, and we both sat in his living room. He brought two bottles of beer, opened them, and gave me one. As I sipped and talked about how the day had been, I mentioned my issue. "Mohan, I want to tell you something very important." "Go ahead. What is it?" Mohan said. "I want to visit my mother in Benin. You know, when the crackdown happened in Ogoniland, my mother and siblings flee to Benin. We haven't seen one another till date. Samuel, the cook, would be going to Benin tomorrow. I want to go with him so he can take me across the border with him." Mr. Mohan took a sip of his beer, looked at me for about 3 seconds, put his glass down, then got up and went into his bedroom. Mohan stayed there for more than 10 minutes. When he came back, he had an envelope, a photo camera, a business card, and a pair of black-cover diaries with shining metals at the four edges. The diary was new and beautiful. Mohan handed over all the items in his hand to me. Before he did, he said, "I know you are leaving and not coming back, but what I don't know is where you're going. When you get to where you are going, call me. I'd tell you what to do." Mohan said this as he handed the items to me. I was stunned and speechless. I sat there looking like a dummy. "I went to Germany when I was 20 years old," Mohan said, sitting back in his seat. We continued with our beer till the session won out. Inside the envelope was my salary and some extra amount he added to it. The next day came. Samuel knocked on my door and let me know he was ready. I rose, used the bathroom, and followed him off till we got to the point of crossing at the Benin/Nigeria border.

Mere border crossing for the first time may not be that significant, but what happened after the crossing made March 1st, 1996, a forever significant day in my life. As we were crossing the border, the eyes of the customs and immigration officers were all over me, but I maintained a straight face, avoiding eye contact. When we got to the Benin side, the driver of the taxi we were in was about to move but the immigration officer asked him to stop. "Hey, you!" The officer sounded, pointing at me. "Where are you going? Come out." My heart jumped almost to my mouth. About to get off the car, my accomplice spoke in French with the officer. "Go back in." The officer ordered. The driver zoomed off. Nobody in the vehicle said a word till we arrived in Cotonou, the country's capital. As Samuel and I walked away from the vehicle, I thought we were going toward another vehicle that would take us to our destination. That wasn't the case. Samuel raced away from me and hopped into a loading vehicle that was waiting for one passenger to complete up. The vehicle drove off. I was left alone and stranded. When that happened, I felt a profound sense of isolation and vulnerability in a foreign land. The unfamiliar sounds and sights of the bustling city only amplified my loneliness, making every step feel heavy with uncertainty. Grappling with the language I could not understand, the distance I had come, indifferent faces of strangers in the vast and unwelcome landscape, my heart ached with a deep sense of abandonment and despair. I kept on walking, looking for the comfort of familiar voices and the embrace of loved ones. I saw an open roadside bar, I walked inside and took a seat almost immediately, with my heart racing up and down.

While sitting, a light-skinned girl walked by. "Hey, excuse me." I holla. The girl stopped. "Do you speak English?" I asked. "Only un peu un peu (meaning, small, small)." The girl said. "Do you know where the Nigerian embassy is located here in the city?" "Ehm no. Only Ambassade de France." "You mean France Embassy…?" I inferred. "Yes, yes." She nodded. "Okay, write the address for me," I said in a somewhat aggressive mode. The girl wrote it. With that piece of paper, I stepped outside and flagged down a motorbike. I showed the bike operator the piece of paper, the guy raced off. I flagged down another one, and that one asked me to get on. He took me to the France Embassy. There, I asked the security officer at the gate if he knew where the Nigerian Embassy was located. In my mind, I thought if I got there, I would be safe. That was not going to be so. "Are you Ogoni?" The police officer asked. "Yes, I am." On hearing that, the officer shook his head, saying no, no, don't go there. He then beckoned the bike man and spoke in dialect to him.

I did not know what the officer told the bike man until we arrived at the American Embassy.

At the Embassy, I accosted the officer at the gate and introduced myself and where I was coming from. The officer beckoned the bike man and used dialect in the communication. I did not understand until we arrived at the UN office. Alighting from the bike, I walked to the security window and introduced myself to the security officer, and he asked if I was from Ogoni. "Yes," I replied. "Come this way." The officer said, beckoning. "Okay, let me pay the bike man." I returned to the bike man and paid him before walking inside the UN compound.

Inside the compound, I met a group of people crowding under a shaded structure in the right-hand corner of the compound. They were all Ogonis. For the first time after the event on January 4th, I met some familiar faces. I was once again in the embrace of friends and loved ones. When Nimi came to hug me, I was filled with emotion so much that tears started streaming down my cheeks. "When did you get here?" I asked, holding her hand, remembering how I helped her out of the muddy gutter she fell into on January 4th. I was so emotional that I couldn't hold a conversation. On the left corner of the compound, a meticulously maintained garden offers a tranquil escape, featuring native plants and a small fountain that provides a soothing soundtrack. I did not get inside the building till after two weeks of staying outside under the shaded structure and taking a bath behind the building before six o'clock in the morning. The building itself is a modern, imposing structure that stands as a beacon of international cooperation amidst the bustling cityscape. The building's sleek, glass façade reflects the vibrant hues of the African sky, symbolizing transparency and openness. When it was my turn to be interviewed by the Protection Officer, Madam Fontus, I had the opportunity to see the inside of the building. Inside, the lobby is an expensive, airy space filled with natural light, adorned with flags of member nations and local artworks that celebrate Benin's rich cultural heritage.

The atmosphere is a blend of quiet efficiency and welcoming warmth, with staff members from diverse backgrounds working together in harmony. Painted light blue and white color, the UN office in Cotonou embodies the spirit of unity and progress, dedicated to addressing regional challenges and fostering sustainable development. After two weeks and 3 days, and after everyone had been interviewed and vetted, we were all transferred to a remote place in a rural area called "Comẽ," where the camp was located.

CHAPTER 15

THE REFUGEE CAMP

The refugee camp sprawled out a patchwork quilt of makeshift tents and tarps, each one telling a silent story of loss and survival. Amidst the sea of faces, young NdaaBari clutched a tattered soccer ball, the last remnant of his childhood before the world turned upside down.

"Mama, when will we go home?" asked little DornuBari, her voice barely rising above the din of the crowded camp. Her mother's eyes, weary yet hopeful, searched the horizon as if willing to reveal their future. As night fell on the camp, Dominic lay awake, the echoes of his once vibrant village haunting the silence between heartbeats. The camp's central well, once a beacon of communal gathering, now stood as a testament to the resilience of displaced people, drawing more than water with each pail hoisted. The laughter of children playing soccer in the dust clashed with the somber reality that surrounded them, a fleeting escape from the gravity of their existence.

In the morning, the scent of frying plantains would waft through the camp, and on the food-sharing day, the scent of frying ice fish would also waft through the camp, creating a bittersweet reminder of home that lingered in the air, as tangible as the memories it conjured. Life in the refugee camp was not without hope and despair as each sunrise brought with it a duality of hope for a happy return to Ogoniland and the despair of another day marked by the sun's relentless journey across the sky.

The culture was one thing the Ogoni people did not let go of no matter the situation. In the evenings, the elders would gather the children, their voices weaving tales of Ogoni folklore, stitching the fabric of their culture tighter with each word spoken. In one session, Mene, 20, stood up, his gaze steadfast. "This is not the end," he whispered to the wind, "Our roots run deeper than the oil that taints our land." Tears, accompanied by emotion, welled up in my eyes. Instantly, every episode of what happened back home began to play in my head.

I took a leave from the session. On my way, I ran into Nimi. "Hey Nonu, are you okay?" Nimi greeted me. "No, I'm not," was my response. "I understand," Nimi said. "I think I may want to leave this camp," I said. "No." "Do not leave. It would be okay, not now, but someday." "I am just too tired of being angry. Staying here will continue to bring up the events back home in my head. I do not want to live like this." I vented. "Remember how you calmed me down at the memorial after the executions of the Nine, and I listened?" Nimi reminded me. That reminder hit me in the chest like a thud. "Well, Nimi, you know I'm too young to be here grappling with the harsh realities of life?" "I know, Nonu," Nimi said. Continuing, Nimi further said, "You know, you've come this far, so, you have to do everything possible to create a better future for yourself despite the challenges we face here." "What do you mean, create a better future? Where is the future here? Resettlement is not coming, if we were to have a resettlement, then, you can talk about creating a better future." I spoke in a somewhat angry tone. "But how are you going to get the resettlement if you leave the camp? Nimi questioned. The question was a food for thought to me. "Well, I will see how it goes. Thank you for the concern, though." "You're welcome. Love you!" Nimi said. "Love you too!!" I said as we both parted ways. It was the first time we have ever ended our conversations with "Love you." "Oh, I forgot, you know we are having visitors from Cotonou coming here tomorrow?" Nimi informed me. "Really? I do not know anything about visitors coming in tomorrow." I said in response. "Yeh, some people from the Interior Office will be here tomorrow." She confirmed. "Okay, we see them when they arrive here," I said and walked off. It made me kind of have different thoughts—deep thoughts, I would say, about this girl. "Nimi, we always run into each other. Mhhhh…" I reflected, walking to my dilapidated tent. Initially, it was four of us in the tent, but later, the other three members went to live with relatives in the camp, leaving me alone by myself. As the camp policy goes, if you are alone in a tent and the tent becomes dilapidated, you stand the chance of not having it replaced. And that was my situation.

As Nimi informed, a group of diplomatic teams from the Benin Interior Ministry, led by one Mr. Randolph, arrived at camp the next day. The team's mission was to convince the Ogoni refugees to return home, alleging that there had been peace back home. The leader, Mr. Randolph, told the murmuring crowd, "Your leader Ledum Mitee has returned home and he's Safe at home. Abacha is dead and you have no reason to be in the refugee camp anymore." In response, the hungry and angry-looking crowd murmured out loudly. In response to the murmuring, Randolph again told the crowd in a somewhat angry tone, "You people just want to go to America, right? Let me tell you, America has its problems, Canada has its problem. All these countries you people are looking forward to going have their problems just like Nigeria." At the time, Nigeria was using the Benin government against the Ogoni refugees, claiming to the international communities that Nigeria has no refugee situation in the country. Ogoni knows this fact. So, when Mr. Randolph made those annoying comments, the Ogoni people wasted no time to respond. The air in the hall grew heavy with an uneasy murmuring.

"We are here laying on mats on a hard floor doing nothing to sustain ourselves. The children have been out of school for a very long time. They need to go somewhere they can be useful. The Nigerian government is telling lies that there is peace at home. If some of us here return home, we can be arrested and thrown into a detention cell. So, even if it is a fact that America has a problem if the country had indicated interest in granting us asylum, the Benin government should allow us to go there." Mr. Borbee, who spoke on behalf of the Ogoni people, told the team.

As soon as the Ogoni spokesperson stopped speaking, slowly, individuals began to disperse, moving toward the exits with a mixture of resignation and trepidation. An elderly woman, leaning on a wooden cane, shook her head as she shuffled past the Officials, her lips pursed tightly in disapproval. Nearby, a young man lingered, his eyes darting around as if searching for an unseen reassurance before he reluctantly turned to leave. Groups of friends and families huddled together, whispering hurriedly, their faces a tapestry of doubt and forced resolve. Children clung to their parents, sensing the unease in the air, their innocent eyes wide with confusion. Bit by bit, the hall emptied, the faint echoes of their footsteps and subdued conversations the only remnants of the once crowded space, now left with the haunting question of what truly awaited them back home.

CHAPTER 16

NONU'S TRIP TO GHANA

For two weeks, I lay on the cold, hard floor of my dark, dilapidated tent, staring at the tattered canvas above me. The flickering shadows cast by the distant light played on the fabric, creating shapes that danced like ghosts of my past. I thought about the non-promising resettlement, the future, a vast unknown stretching before me like an uncharted desert. Dreams of becoming a better person, of helping at least my community, felt both painfully close and impossibly distant. The whispers of the dead, and of my family, echoed in my mind, urging me to hold onto hope. The image of Sorko Gbinee, laying naked and dead in ashes with his head turned backward, served as beacon in the dark, a promise to myself that someday, I would turn my dreams into reality. the thought of leaving and Nimi's advice not to leave continued to clash inside of me. Conditions on the camp are becoming harder and harsher by the day. The once-a-month little portion of the Red Cross rationed food items were not enough. With all this, life in camp was becoming tough. And it only got worse on the night storm blew away the entire already dilapidated tent and placed it distance away while I was still inside.

It was food sharing day. Earlier in the day, the sun was disappearing, a sign that a severe storm was looming. I got my rations and put everything but the fresh ice fish together and made them my pillow. So, when the storm took away my tent, I just whisked my food items with my right hand and walked through the rain to a block building across. I was standing under a shade from the rain when Singto came and asked me to sleep in the tent he shared with others. None of the other members refused me. I spent the rest of the night in there till it was morning.

Bittered by what happened to my tent, the general deteriorating conditions in the camp, and the opportunities for resettlement seeming bleak, I made the difficult decision to leave the camp in search of a better life. Driven by desperation and hope, I embarked on a perilous journey to Ghana, facing numerous obstacles and dangers along the way. Upon reaching Ghana, I encountered a new set of challenges as I attempted to navigate life in a foreign country. I grappled with the issues of identity, discrimination, and economic hardship, all while clinging to the hope of a brighter future. After months of uncertainty and struggle, I reached a pivotal moment of reckoning where I must confront the reality of my situation. Despite the allure of staying in Ghana, I ultimately decided to return to the refugee camp, realizing that my chances of resettlement to the United States were slim without proper documentation and support.

But there are moments I wouldn't forget while on the streets of Acra, Ghana. As one can see, out on the streets creates the possibility of running into all and any kind of person. And that's exactly what happened to Nonu. In one of his moments on the streets, Nonu met Erasmos, a 44-year-old, six feet and three inches tall man from Ghana, deported from Europe on account of drug dealings. As the sun dipped below the horizon, casting the city's streets in the amber glow of streetlights, Nonu and the man, who he simply called Erasmos, began their nightly wander through Acra – particularly the Kwame Nkuruma Circle area. The air was heavy with the scent of roasting plantains and jollof rice wafting from roadside vendors, mingling with the musty smell of the streets. Every evening, they met at the old colonial clock tower that stood silent and stoic in the city center, its arms frozen at twelve.

Nonu listened with mixed fascination and trepidation as Erasmos regaled him with tales from Paris. Erasmos' voice would rise and fall like the crescendos of a tragic opera, painting vivid pictures of smoky underground clubs, perilous drug deals, and fleeting romances with women young enough to be his daughters. Despite his sordid past, there was something magnetic about Erasmos' charisma, an allure that drew Nonu deeper into his stories each night.

The two men roamed from corner to corner, their footsteps echoing through the narrow alleyways lined with shuttered stalls and dimly lit bars. They walked past the bustling Makola Market, now quiet after a day of frenzied trading, the only sounds being the occasional bark of a stray dog or the far-off hum of a generator. Nonu often felt a sense of camaraderie with the shadows that clung to the walls; both were silent witnesses to the secrets and stories of the night.

One evening, as they sat on a crumbling stone bench in an abandoned park, the conversation shifted. Erasmos revealed that he was expecting some money. His eyes gleamed with the promise of a better tomorrow. Nonu, ever the optimist, shared his own dreams—of returning to Lagos a successful man, of reuniting with his family, of finding a place he could finally call home. Erasmos listened, nodding thoughtfully, his face unreadable in the half-light.

When the money came, Erasmos kept his word. He handed Nonu a thick wad of 40,000 cedis, a small fortune by their standards. Nonu was overwhelmed with gratitude, his mind racing with the possibilities this windfall presented. Little did he know this act of generosity would soon be overshadowed by betrayal.

Nonu cherished a big black, weathered diary with shining metal at its four edges that his Indian boss in Lagos had given him. Nonu always carrying it along, and it was his most prized possession, filled with sketches, notes, and memories too precious to forget. The diary held a piece of Nonu's soul, a tangible link to his past and a beacon for his future. Prior before Erasmos' money came in, the man advised Nonu to keep the diary in the ceiling at the central post office in the Great Kwame Nkuruma Circle in Acra Central. The very morning that would be the last time to see Erasmos, Nonu reached out to retrieve it from the post office, only to find it missing. Panic set in. He searched frantically throughout the post office, but all to no avail. His heart pounding against his ribs.

Erasmos' face flashed in his mind. "Only he knew about the diary's importance, and he was the one who advised me to keep it at the place that I kept it." Nonu thought. Then, a sinking feeling settled in Nonu's stomach as he realized the truth. Betrayal stung sharper than any blade. The man whom he had regarded as a brother had stolen not just his diary, but a part of his soul. Nonu felt an emptiness that the 40,000 cedis could never fill. Anguish gave way to anger and sadness; how could a friend do this? Erasmos was nowhere to be found. He was gone and gone for life.

In the days that followed, Nonu wandered the streets alone,

haunted by memories of the lost diary and the tales Erasmos had told, more so, was how he narrated how he used to make fake documents for newly arrived immigrants in Europe. The diary contained Nonus's refugee documents, some of which enabled him crossed Benin/Togo and the Togo/Ghana boarder. Night after night, he visited their usual haunts, secretly hoping to see Erasmos and demand answers, but the man had vanished as suddenly as he had appeared. Acra, in all its chaotic beauty, felt colder and lonelier. Nonu vowed never to let anyone close again, to guard his heart as fiercely as he once guarded his diary.

Life went on, but the streets of Acra felt different without Erasmos by his side. The betrayal had left a scar, a reminder of the fickle nature of trust and friendship. As he roamed the city, the whispers of his lost diary echoed in his mind, a ghost of past hopes and dreams that had slipped through his fingers like sand. But that wasn't the only mysterious thing that happened to Nonu on the streets of Acra.

One day, around Easther, as Nonu narrated, I stood at my usual spot in the central post office at Kwame Nkuruma Circle of Acra, Ghana, a location bustling with people making international phone calls. This place had become more than just a usual hangout for me; it was where I felt connected to the world outside. On this particular day, the air buzzed with an unusual excitement. Two large buses pulled up, and a wave of American exchange students disembarked, their faces alight with curiosity and excitement.

I watched with keen interest as the students made their way toward the phone booths. My curiosity peaked, noting how the Liberian guys, who typically occupied the post office, swarmed around the female students, vying for their attention, while the male students were largely ignored.

I observed the scene with the intensity of a hawk, knowing that any moment might bring an encounter rich with stories and new experiences. It wasn't long before one of the male students noticed my watchful presence and approached me. As I saw him coming, I braced myself as the student, a tall guy with glasses and a wide, friendly smile, asked, "Hey, where are you from?"

"I am from Ogoni, the land of Ken Saro-Wiwa," I replied with a mix of pride and caution, half-expecting a nod of recognition. Instead, the student's reaction was startling. His expression instantly became distressed, and he burst out, "They blame us for the killing of Ken Saro-Wiwa!" His voice was loud enough to draw the attention of everyone in the vicinity. The bustling atmosphere of the post office came to a halt as people turned to witness the unfolding drama.

I was taken aback by the outburst. My initial surprise quickly turned to confusion and a slight sense of shame, though I had no reason to feel guilty. After a tense few moments, the student, realizing the commotion he had caused, calmed down and, in a gesture that took me by surprise, handed me a $10 note as an apology or perhaps a peace offering.

"Here, take this. I'm sorry for the outburst," the student said, still visibly shaken. I accepted the note with a nod, appreciative yet confused by the turn of events. With the money, I decided to buy a new shirt, a small but meaningful gesture to myself. The shirt, bright and colorful, felt like a piece of new hope amid the chaos of the post office incident.

Days turned into weeks, and life continued at its steady pace. One afternoon, feeling unusually tired, I decided to take a nap, using my cherished new shirt to cover myself. It was a breezy day, and the comfort of the shirt provided a sense of security as I drifted off to sleep. When I awoke, however, my security blanket was gone. The shirt had been stolen.

A wave of emotions washed over me: disbelief, anger, and a profound sense of loss. The shirt was not just a piece of clothing; it symbolized an unexpected connection, an experience that had rattled me but also made me feel seen and acknowledged. Its theft felt personal, a cruel reminder of my vulnerable position in the world.

Since the incident at the post office, the authorities had grown more stringent. The security personnel no longer allowed anyone to sleep there, disrupting the sense of community and sanctuary I had relied on. I felt a mixture of resentment and resignation. The post office, which had once been a vibrant hub of interaction and safety, now felt antagonistic and cold.

I continued to wander the streets of Acra, avoiding where my shirt once lay. I reminisced about the student, the unexpected chaos, and the brief moment of connection across different worlds. Though troubled by the recent events, I resolved to move forward, finding solace in the belief that new opportunities and experiences awaited me beyond the post office walls.

Yet, the memory of that bright, stolen shirt lingered, a symbol of fleeting kindness and the unpredictable nature of his life. And I swore to reclaim that sense of connection and hope, even as I faced an uncertain future.

With some money from the $10 left, I decided to pay for a shower one bright morning. When I arrived at the shower service place, I decided to wash the one last t-shirt on me. I had finished washing the T-shirt when loud music sounded out nearby. Feeling very curious about the loud sound of music, I hurriedly took the shower and grabbed my t-shirt, even when not dried, put it on, and headed toward the direction where the music was coming from. When I got there, it was something bigger than I thought. Different NGOs in Accra had come together to organize an Easter celebration for those on the street. There was food to eat, water to drink, and the food was to be served by Miss Ghana. There was a medical booth to attend to those in need.

First, Lucky Dube, a reggae legend from South Africa, performed at the event. Then the food was served by Miss Ghana. I made sure I got in line quickly so I could be served by Miss Ghana. I was so impressed by what I saw. I had about 50 cedis left on me. With this impression on my mind, I followed what the announcer said. I went to the Lions Club of Ghana booth and donated 25 cedis, leaving me with 25. At the booth, I introduced myself and let them know why I was donating the 25 cedis. The club members were so appreciative of my kind gesture. I was directed from there to go to the medical booth for a check-up. At the medical booth, I was the last in line, but a medical student working there asked me to go to the side. "You, you, step this way," the worker said, pointing to the left where she wanted me to sit.

I became a bit scared as to why she asked me to step aside. After attending to all the people, she called me to her desk. She then interrogated me, and I told her where I was from and how I got here. The girl then gave me an address of a main medical facility and drew a sketch of how to get there. She also gave me her own hostel address and asked me to come and meet her. I did all she asked me to do. On the day to meet her, she surprised me. She gave me an envelope and a sketch map on how to get to her mom. She also gave me 1000 cedis for feeding. I took the envelope to her mother. I didn't read it, and I didn't know what she wrote inside. But after giving the envelope to her mom, the aged woman counted 12 pieces of juice boxes and asked me if I could sell them at the car park.

I said yes, and she let me take the items out of her store. At the park, I hawked the juice boxes and sold all of them. I returned the main capital and kept the gains. I continued doing that until my eyes started deteriorating. Despite my situation, I was filled with a sense of purpose. The support from the volunteers and the unexpected kindness from the medical student gave me hope. I felt inspired to keep pushing forward, even as my eyesight worsened. I felt that Heroes of the Ogoni Struggle spirits and that of the Invisible Victims were guiding me throughout my journey.

It wasn't just about the money or the immediate help I received. It was about the human connection and the realization that people genuinely cared. I endured the challenges, each day becoming a test of my resilience. Sometimes, it felt overwhelming, but I found solace in the small victories. The trust the medical student showed by involving her family opened a new path for me. The aged woman's acceptance and task of selling juice boxes taught me the value of hard work and honesty.

Every bottle sold was a step taken towards self-reliance. My appreciation grew not just for the assistance received, but for the lessons learned. There were days when my vision blurred so badly that every step was an act of faith. Yet, I held on to the memory of the loud music, the celebration, and the hands that reached out to lift me. These memories acted as a beacon, guiding me through the darkness. Eventually, my condition forced me to seek further help. The journey was far from easy, but each moment of gratitude carried me forward. It became evident that endurance is fueled not just by physical strength but by the bonds we form along the way.

My return to the refugee camp was fraught with mixed emotions—relief at being back in familiar surroundings yet tinged with disappointment and uncertainty about the future. I grappled with feelings of failure and disillusionment but also found solace in the resilience of my community and bonds of friendship forged in adversity. However, despite the setbacks and hardships I had endured, I found hope and purpose in my decision to return to the camp. I became a source of inspiration and support for others, sharing experiences and advocating for change within the camp. "Nonu, welcome back!" "How was it?" That was the greeting I received from almost everybody. "Leaving was never an easy choice, but I had to try." "I had to believe there was something better out there." I would say in response. I suddenly turned into a preacher. This was because everyone wanted to hear from me what was my experiences in Ghana. And when that happened, I gave them what they asked for—extra wisdom. I would say: "I felt like a stranger in a strange land, but here, in the camp, I am home." "Returning may seem like a step backward, but it's also a step closer to where I belong—to the possibility of a future worth fighting for." "They say home is where the heart is. Well, my heart is here, among the resilient souls who refused to be defined by their circumstances."

Whenever I said those words, they would laugh hard like they had been looking for it. "Nonu, it looks like you went on a study vacation." Some would tease. "Yes indeed. What I went through in Ghana was like a study vacation, you know?" "Resettlement may be a distant dream, but hope is not lost. If we stand together, we can weather any storm" I would add.

CHAPTER 17

UNDER THE MANGO TREE

Before my journey to Ghana, me and my compatriots used to find space far into the bush where we would sit down, and smoke weed. When I returned, the story was different. The company I left behind had cleared a spot under a mango tree where body and soul meet and haze. This spot offers a temporary escape from the harsh realities of life in the refugee camp. There, not just me, but any visitors to this spot find solace and camaraderie among fellow refugees who share similar struggles and experiences.

Smoking weed under the mango trees becomes a ritualistic bonding experience for me and my companions, fostering a sense of belonging and unity within the community. It serves as a space where we can share stories and laughter and support each other amidst hardships. In moments of solitude amidst the haze of smoke, I would reflect on my journey, my hopes, and my dreams for the future. The weed spot was like a sanctuary where I could process thoughts and emotions away from the noise and chaos of the camp. To me, underneath the mango tree was special because, here, I found a moment of peace amidst the chaos. In the smoke, I see glimpses of a future, beyond the fences that surround the camp, where freedom and opportunity await. Here, among the whispers of the wind and the rustle of leaves, I find solace in the company of kindred spirits. In the haze of the moment, our burdens feel lighter, our laughter louder, as we forge bonds stronger than steel. Underneath this canopy of stars, we share stories of survival, resilience, and the unwavering hope that fuels our journey forward. The other day, I had just finished a morning session and was returning to the camp. Eyes all red. I was stoned to the brim and stinking weed odor. The last person I was hoping to see was Nimi. But lo and behold, there she was, coming out of the gate while I was going through the gate to get inside the camp. Nimi smelled the pungent odor of weed on me and pulled me aside for talks.

"Nonu, come, come, come." Nimi called, pulling me to the side for a talk. "Oh, so what I was told that you smoke weed is true?" With the mood I was in, I couldn't fathom what she was saying. "What…what's it?" I stuttered. "So, what if I smoke weed?" I managed to answer the question in defense. "Well, I am going to the market now. When I return, we talk. Would you eat my soup today?" "Oh yeah! I've been wanting to eat your soup a long time ago." I said, lovingly. "You're crazy, do you know that?" She commented, tossing my hand from side to side. Of course, I know myself better than you." I allegedly responded. "You know in a month; I'd be traveling to the States?" Nimi informed. "Yes, I do," I answered. "I know you won't even remember me when you get there, so, it doesn't bother me." "Oh no! Why do you think so?" Nimi exclaimed. "Because I know so," I replied. We both stood hand in hand without words for seconds before she let go of my hand and proceeded on.

The thoughts of building a relationship with Nimi increasingly overwhelmed me. This is because, in her eyes, I see a reflection of everything I long for—hope, beauty, and a future beyond the camp. So, when Nimi finally gained resettlement and traveled to the U.S., I carried her memory with me like a beacon of light, guiding me through the darkness of uncertainty and longing. Almost a year passed, no sign of Nimi, no calls, no words, nothing. The only place I would see and talk to Nimi was in the land of dreams, where I searched for her among the faces in the crowd, hoping for a chance to rewrite our story. When I finally gained resettlement to the U.S, I was relieved with the thought that I would meet Nimi, and we could both rekindle our relationship. That did not happen during our reunion. Our reunion feels like fate's gentle nudge, yet the distance between us feels wider than ever, bridged only by the echoes of what could have been. As I watch her walk away, I carry with me the bittersweet reminder that some connections are meant to be cherished from afar.

CHAPTER 18

RESETTLEMENT

Nonu sat in the shade of an old canvas tent, tracing invisible patterns in the dusty ground. The days in the refugee camp had a timeless quality, each one blending into the next with monotonous regularity. News traveled fast here, often more quickly than the scarce supplies or the occasional letters from afar. Yet, this day was different. The camp's tension was palpable, like the static in the air before a storm.

Word had spread of a list—names of families approved for resettlement to the USA. Nonu's pulse quickened as he overheard snippets of conversations. Children, for once, seemed quieter, their eyes wide with curiosity as their parents clustered in anxious groups around the camp office. The sun beat down mercilessly, but no one moved from their spot, expecting the life-changing announcement.

When Nonu's name was called, it felt surreal, as though it was meant for someone else. He stood frozen, the weight of hope and uncertainty pinning him to the ground. His heart pounded in his chest, and he barely registered the excited murmurs around him.

The people who had become his makeshift family—fellow refugees who shared their stories, their fears, and their dreams—were now reaching out to him with congratulatory hugs and teary smiles.

The air in the camp shifted, a mix of celebration and melancholy. For every family selected, some remained, their hopes deferred. Nonu could see it in their eyes, a blend of joy for him and sorrow for themselves. He felt it deeply, the bittersweet reality of survival and the privilege of being chosen.

As he walked back to his tent, the gravity of his new reality began to settle in. The journey to the USA promised a chance for a future he had only dared to dream of—a life free from the confines of the camp, marked by opportunities for his future children, safety, and a fresh start. Yet, he also felt a pang of guilt, leaving behind the camaraderie and the shared struggles that had defined his existence for so long.

On camp, children sensed the change and clung to their parents, their youthful exuberance tempered by the gravity of the news. Mrs. Nzebee hugged her children tightly, her mind racing with thoughts of wardrobes filled with clothes and schools equipped with chalkboards and books. It was overwhelming, the idea of starting over in a land so foreign and vast.

In the evening, the camp echoed with a cacophony of emotions. As night fell, I lay down, staring at the dark, star-specked sky. There was excitement within me, bubbling up with the promise of the unknown. Yet, the stars seemed to whisper the stories of those I would leave behind—their dreams still tethered to the dusty ground beneath me.

"Tomorrow, preparations would begin." I thought to myself. "There would be paperwork, briefings, and goodbyes." "But I'm resolved to face it all with a heart full of gratitude." I thought.

The USA was a new horizon, a beacon of hope. As I closed my eyes, I whispered a silent prayer for myself, for those who remained, and for the journey ahead. The camp wasn't just a place; it had been a crucible of resilience. "Come what may, I vowed to carry that strength into my new life, honoring the past while stepping boldly into my future," I said to myself and fell asleep.

Despite the unpleasant nature of the camp, there was still something good that came out of it. The camp provided me with the opportunity to meet several emerging heroes of the Ogoni struggle. These emerging heroes turned out to be activists who played some key roles in the Ogoni fight for justice. Some became members of the National Union of Ogoni Students (NUOS-USA). This student arm of MOSOP played an active role in bringing Shell to the Dutch Court for masterminding the devastation of Ogoniland and the murder of acclaimed writer and activist Ken Saro-Wiwa. Shell settled the case out of court with the sum of 15 million U.S. dollars. To me, that was a victory. NUOS also petitioned the UN Environmental Unit to investigate the devastation of Ogoniland and to conduct an impact assessment on Ogoniland. When the assessment was done, the result was staggering. The UN Environmental Impact Assessment Program reported that the level of benzene in the groundwater in Ogoniland, due to the devastations caused by oil spills, was 900 times above the World Health Organization (WHO) guidelines, a report that vindicated Ken Saro-Wiwa and the Ogoni People.

Heroes of the Ogoni struggle inspired people around the world to stand up to corporate exploitation and devastation of their land. The restoration of the Ogoni environment is not done yet. The fight for justice is not over, either. And under the vast, indigo sky, the Ogoni lands lay scarred yet alive, a testament to the unyielding spirit of a people bound by their love for each other and their land. As the children played around the sacred tree, their laughter intermingling with the winds of change, it was clear that the seeds of the struggle had taken root in fertile ground. The heroes of the Ogoni struggle had forged a path not just for themselves, but for generations to come, ensuring that their voices would echo in the annals of history, a story of resilience and hope.

After months of uncertainty and anticipation, the moment Nonu had been waiting for finally arrived. Stepping off the plane and inhaling for the first time the crisp air of a foreign land, he felt a mixture of relief, excitement, and trepidation. The bustling environment of the airport contrasted sharply with the quiet resilience of his homeland. As he navigated through the unfamiliar yet strangely ordered chaos, Nonu couldn't help but recall the faces of those he'd left behind—faces that had etched themselves deeply into his heart.

Living as a resettled refugee in the United States was a mosaic of challenges and new beginnings. Nonu faced the immediate task of learning a new way of life—one dictated by a frenetic pace, complicated systems, and the necessity to constantly code-switch between his cultural identity and this new world. English, which had once been an academic exercise, became his lifeline, the bridge to communicating his past and present. It felt surreal to converse freely without fear of retribution, yet it also made him acutely aware of the silence imposed on those still fighting back home. Each day, he marveled at the opportunities around him. Here, he could speak openly, share his story publicly, and advocate without the looming shadow of repression. Yet, despite these newfound freedoms, Nonu's heart ached with an immutable sorrow for the Ogoni people he had left behind. Their struggle was far from over, their voices still muffled beneath layers of oppression. Nonu threw himself into his studies, determined to make the most of this second chance. Knowledge, he believed, was the ultimate weapon in his ongoing fight for justice. Engaging with activists and scholars, he began documenting the plight of his people, bringing to light stories that had been forcibly kept in the dark. His narrative became a beacon, drawing attention to the invisible victims who continued to endure so much. Some nights, when the loneliness became too heavy to bear, Nonu would sit by his window, gazing at the expanse of the American skyline, and remember the rivers and forests of his homeland. He would recall the songs of resistance, the whispered conversations filled with fear and hope, and the faces of martyrs who had fallen in the fight for freedom. These memories, bittersweet and sacred, fueled his resolve.

Nonu understood that resettlement was not the end of his journey but merely a new beginning. His presence in the U.S.A. was a testament to the resilience of his people, a continuation of the struggle from a different battleground. With every step forward, he carried with him the weight of their hopes and dreams, dedicating his achievements to those whose voices had been silenced. In this land of new beginnings, Nonu found his purpose—to be a bridge between two worlds, to make visible the invisible, and to ensure that the struggle of the Ogoni people would never be forgotten.

As dawn broke over the verdant expanse of Ogoniland, the air hummed with a renewed sense of hope, mingling with the echoes of past struggles. Nkata and Mbane stood together at the edge of their village, watching as the sun's rays kissed the treetops, illuminating the path that their forefathers had courageously trodden. The victory they had fought so tirelessly for was now within reach, a testament to their indomitable spirit and unwavering solidarity.

The multinational corporations, once indifferent to the cries of the Ogoni people, had finally been held accountable. With international scrutiny and an unprecedented unity amongst the diverse ethnicities of Nigeria, reparations were made. Soil remediation projects began, led by scientists who were not just experts, but also allies in the fight for justice. Rivers once blackened with oil were slowly beginning to show signs of life. Fish, an integral part of the Ogoni diet and culture, were returning, symbolizing the restoration of both environment and community.

The elders, no longer haunted by the fear of displacement, gathered to share stories of the fallen heroes whose sacrifices paved the way for this momentous change. Ken Saro-Wiwa's name was spoken with reverence, his vision of a free Ogoniland now blossoming from the seeds of resistance he had sown. Nkata felt a swell of pride as she recalled her own father's resilience, his legacy now secures in the minds of the new generation. A resettlement program was done for those who fled to a refugee camp, offering new homes to those displaced by the ferocious life-changing tactics of the past. The young and old alike were returning, bringing with them the promise of renewal. Children, unburdened by the guilt and pain of their ancestors, played freely in the rejuvenated fields, their laughter a sweet symphony of healing. Mbonmene, with the wisdom of years etched in his eyes, turned to Nkata. "The struggle has not ended. It has merely transformed," he said. "Our fight now is to protect this land, to guard these victories, and to ensure that our story is not just remembered but learned from."

Nkata nodded, feeling the weight of responsibility mingling with hope. She knew that the scars of the past would always mark their history, but they would not define it. Standing firm in a land once ravaged by greed, the Ogoni people had reclaimed their narrative, shifting it from one of sorrow to resilience, from invisibility to a beacon of justice. As the sun climbed higher, the village erupted in celebration. Drums beat rhythmically, echoing the heartbeat of a community that had not just survived, but thrived. Women adorned in vibrant fabrics danced, their movements narrating stories of defiance and triumph. Men raised their voices in harmonious chants, honoring the undying spirit of their people.

In this moment of unity and joy, Nkata whispered a prayer for all the heroes—both known and invisible—who had given so much. She vowed to continue their legacy, ensuring that their sacrifices were never in vain. With determination carved into her soul, she embraced Kakateh, both standing as symbols of an Ogoniland that would never again be silenced. The struggle had given birth to a resilience that could not be extinguished. And as the day progressed, the Ogoni people forged ahead, their spirits intertwined with the land they loved fiercely, living as vigilant stewards of a hard-won peace.

CHAPTER 19

THE AMERICA'S PROBLEMS

Nonu stepped off the plane with the words of Mr. Randolph in his mind. Mr. Randolph, the representative of the Benin Government had told the Ogoni refugees that "America has problems," and those words were echoing in Nonu's head. He took a deep breath of the fresh American air. He had imagined this moment countless times, dreaming of the land of opportunity and freedom. Yet, as he navigated through the bustling airport, a sense of unease began to creep in. Over and over, the diplomat's words to the Ogoni refugees in Benin echoed in his mind: "America has problems."

His first glimpse of these problems came almost immediately. Outside the airport, he saw rows of homeless people lining the streets. Makeshift tents and cardboard boxes served as their homes. Nonu had heard about the wealth of America, but this stark reality contradicted everything he had been told.

As he traveled further into the city, Nonu noticed the extreme contrasts. Skyscrapers loomed over dilapidated buildings, and luxury cars zoomed past beggars. The disparities were glaring. He found it hard to reconcile these images with the America of his dreams. Nonu's new apartment was empty except for the cooking stove and a refrigerator. Worst still, it was in a neighborhood plagued by crime and poverty. The walls were thin, and he often heard arguments and sirens throughout the night. It was a far cry from the safe- haven he had envisioned. Determined to understand more, Nonu started reading local newspapers and watching the news. The headlines were filled with stories of political unrest, social inequality, and racial tensions. Protests erupted in various cities, demanding justice and change. The diplomat's words were proving true in every step of the way, but the heroes of the Ogoni struggle spirits were also talking to him.

At his new job, Nonu encountered colleagues from diverse backgrounds, each with their own stories of struggle. One coworker, Maria, confided in him about the challenges of being an immigrant in America. Another, James, spoke about the systemic racism he faced daily. Nonu listened, his heart heavy with the weight of their words. He soon realized that America, like every other country, had its own set of problems. The illusion of a perfect society shattered, revealing a complex and multifaceted reality. Nonu's journey had just begun, and he was determined to understand these problems deeply, hoping one day to contribute to the solutions. What Nonu would learn later in his days, weeks, months, and years of living in America would certainly shatter his hope of contributing to any solutions that would end the 'America's problems.'

One late morning at his restaurant job, the lunchtime rush was buzzing around them. The clinking of cutlery, the hum of conversation, and the occasional burst of laughter that every employee seemed to enjoy turned out meaningless to Nonu after hearing what came out of his manager's mouth. Talking to some of his white employees, the manager said:

"I wish I could put Jessy Jackson and Bill Clinton in an airplane and crash it into ocean."

Shocked to his bone, Nonu stared at his manager, disbelief painted across his face. Those chilling words that his manager had just said with an offhanded nonchalance made Nonu's blood run cold. Nonu had always considered America a land of opportunities and dreams, a place where hard work could propel anyone to success. But that one sentence shattered his illusion of unity and progress. As he arranged plates and refilled drinks, his mind swirled with questions. Why such hatred? What did Clinton and Jackson do to warrant such a statement?

Later, during his break, Nonu slipped into the small, cluttered staff room. He pulled out his phone and started researching. He read about the civil rights struggles that Jessy Jackson championed, about the political landscapes Clinton navigated. Slowly, the pieces of a larger, more complex puzzle started to fall into place. America wasn't just the land of the free; it was also a battleground of ideologies and power struggles, a place where past and present conflicts simmered just beneath the surface. "But there's nothing here that these men did that would call for such hateful statement." Nonu sat there and pondered with a chilling hand of fear gripping him by the throat.

Nonu's fingers hovered over the screen as he read article after article, each one revealing another layer of tension, division, and history. He learned about systemic racism, political scandals, and deeply ingrained prejudices. It wasn't that he hadn't known problems existed; it was the depth and breadth of these issues that overwhelmed him.

As his shift wound down, Nonu found himself back in the kitchen, wiping down counters and stacking dishes. He glanced at his manager, who was now laughing with a couple of regulars, the earlier venomous statement seemingly forgotten. But Nonu couldn't forget. The manager's words were a stark reminder that the America he admired was also a place grappling with its demons.

That night, as Nonu lay in bed, staring at the cracked ceiling of his small apartment, he felt a weight settle over him. He had come to America to build a future, but he realized now that part of that future would involve not just personal success but understanding and perhaps confronting the deep-seated issues that plagued his new home.

Nonu promised himself that he wouldn't shy away from the harsh realities he had discovered. He would educate himself, speak out when he could, and, above all, remain hopeful that the America he believed in—a place of genuine equality and opportunity—could one day become a reality for everyone.

It was a new week in February. That afternoon, Nonu resumed his shift with a free and open mind. He had managed to leave the event of the previous week behind. His restaurant was to host a group of African-America celebrating Dr. MLK birthday. Preparations for the evening dinner were at the final stage. And what Nonu was about to witness would negatively alter the day's shift for him.

Nonu's hands trembled as he pushed open the wooden door to the private dining room where the fruit tray buffet had been meticulously arranged. The wafting scent of ripe melons, tangy citrus, and creamy bananas greeted him, a sharp contrast to the bile rising in his throat. They had poured their hearts into this spread; every slice, every arrangement was a testament to their respect and admiration for Dr. Martin Luther King Jr.'s legacy.

But as his eyes adjusted from the dim hallway to the brightly lit room, the serene satisfaction he anticipated feeling was shattered. His breath caught, and for a moment, time itself seemed to bend and stretch in grotesque slow motion. There, atop the splendid buffet, one of his white colleagues was performing an abhorrent pantomime. The man's oversized boots smeared across the carefully arranged fruit, and he mimicked spewing, his face contorted into a mockery of disgust and disdain. The juices of crushed strawberries and mangled melons pooled beneath his soles, mingling in a lurid stain of desecration. It was a heartbreaking scene for Nonu. He almost broke down in tears.

Nonu's immediate instinct was to shout, to rush forward and pull this person away from the sacred spread, but his body betrayed him, paralyzing him in place. His mind raced back to the countless hours spent preparing this; every slice of pineapple, every artful display of berries designed to honor the importance and joy of the occasion. His heart pounded, each beat a painful reminder of the historical weight of the day, now crushed under the vulgarity of such a deliberate insult.

Who was this man to defile what was meant to be a respectful and celebration? The ugliness of racism was something taught to Nonu through the history books and civil rights stories his mother recited with a voice laden with sorrow and resilience. Yet here it was, alive and staggering, smoldering like ancient, toxic refuse in the otherwise progressive corridors of their very modern establishment.

The colleague noticed Nonu standing in the doorway, his sneer shifting into a look of bored disdain. "Oh, come on, Nonu," he said, his tone dripping with condescension. "It's just a joke."

A joke. The words ignited a fire within Nonu, finally spurring his feet into motion. He took a step, then another, but the chasm of ethical and moral distance between them felt insurmountable. His voice, usually calm and composed, came out as a strangled whisper. "Get off the table." The man rolled his eyes but stepped down with exaggerated slowness, his smirk never faltering. He wiped his boots on the tablecloth, leaving dark smudges on the once-crisp white fabric. Nonu forced himself to look away from the ruin of the fruit tray and meet the man's eyes. "You think this is a joke?" he said, his voice gaining strength. "This is about respect. This is about humanity."

The man shrugged, unrepentant. "Whatever, man. It's not a big deal."

But it was a big deal. A very big deal. Nonu knew it, as did anyone with a beating heart and a conscience. This room, this day, signified more than just a celebration; it represented a continuing struggle for dignity and equality. And in this moment, that struggle felt personal. He could see the reflection of countless faces in his mind's eye—friends, family, ancestors—each one deserving of the respect this man had so callously trampled.

Nonu straightened his spine, drawing on the legacy of those who had come before him, those who had endured far worse indignities yet remained unbroken. "Get out," he said, his voice steady now, each syllable forged from steel and fire.

As the man slunk out of the room, Nonu felt the weight of a centuries-old pain settle on his shoulders, but he also felt something else: resolve. There was work to do, today and every day, to honor the legacy of Dr. Martin Luther King Jr., to reclaim the peace and beauty trampled by ignorance and hate. Nonu took a deep breath and turned his attention back to the table, beginning the task of restoring what had been so carelessly defiled. But it didn't end there. Nonu reported the incident to his Assistant Supervisor, who later reported it to the banquet manager. The ignorant white co-worker was fired. Nonu suffered a tremendous hate and name calling when the news of what happened filtered into the ears of other white workers. One evening, Jennifer, a white female bartender, asked Nonu to get her a bucket of ice from the kitchen. As Nonu was about leaving the room to go get the ice, Jennifer called Nonu "Fool."

Nonu could feel the weight of the room shift the moment he stepped back into the dining area with the bucket of ice. The air thickened, heavy with unspoken words and simmering resentment. He could hear Jennifer's dismissive snort even over the clinking of ice cubes, a sound that resonated more deeply than any insult flung directly.

"Can't even do a simple task without making a scene," Jennifer muttered, loudly enough for all near the bar to hear but just low enough to challenge any claim of direct harassment. The laughter that followed her words stung; each chuckle was like a small knife twisted into Nonu's already bruised spirit.

Nonu's grip tightened on the bucket's handle, his knuckles whitening as she struggled to keep her composure. Every loud conversation, every sideways glance felt like a magnifying glass burning into her skin. She placed the ice bucket behind the counter, forcing a smile that she hoped conveyed some semblance of calm professionalism.

"Thanks, Nonu," Jennifer said, the mockery in her tone

unmistakable. For a moment, Nonu met her eyes, and what she saw stole her breath—hatred, pure and raw, layered over a foundation of smug satisfaction. Jennifer was aware that her power extended beyond her position as a bartender, reaching tendrils of influence enveloping their small workplace. Nonu turned away, focusing on refilling the drink dispensers. It was a monotonous task, one that usually provided a sense of routine comfort. Today, it was merely an opportunity for his thoughts to whirl in an ever-darkening spiral.

He replayed the events of the past few days: standing up in the staff meeting, his voice trembling yet firm as he reported what he had seen. The way his manager's eyes had widened in horror at his account, followed swiftly by a stormy silence that promised repercussions. The abruptness with which the guilty co-worker had been led out, the shouts of dismay and protest echoing long after he was gone.

For a brief moment, Nonu had felt a twinge of hope—that perhaps justice had been served, that right actions did matter. But the backlash was swift and merciless. Anonymous notes left in her locker, dripping with venomous words. Acknowledgments from co-workers that became grudging, then nonexistent. The scorn in their eyes, the way conversation died the moment he entered a room.

He had thought Jennifer, at least, might understand. They had shared more than a few late shifts, swapped stories over coffee, and commiserated over the grind of their jobs. But all that had evaporated in the heat of the current hostility, revealing an uglier truth beneath.

Each shift had become a gauntlet. During breaks in the staff room, he found solace only in the quiet—the only time no one else decided to be there, avoiding even the pretense of civility. Nonu would sit with his back to the wall, knees drawn up, a book open but unread in his lap, ears alert to the ambient noise of the restaurant and the muted conversations that never included him.

His thoughts drifted to why he had done it—to the promises he had made to himself and his family, to be a person of integrity no matter the consequences. His grandmother's words echoed in his mind, those wise and weary sayings about the long arc of justice and the price of righteousness. Sitting in the dim break room, he felt the burden of those ideals more keenly than ever before.

Returning to his duties, every task carried an undercurrent of tension. Still, there were moments of pure, restless resistance—small acts of defiance he allowed himself. Straightening his back. Meeting the ridicule head-on with a steady gaze. Refusing to let his voice falter when he had to speak. He wasn't a hero; he was tired, scared, and angry. But he refused to be diminished. Each shift was a battle, and though he bore the scars of silent wounds, his resolve hardened with each passing day.

In the reflection of the mirror behind the bar, he caught his own eye and saw something that Jennifer's sneers could not diminish. Strength. Pain, yes. But also, a defiance that refused to bow under the weight of others' contempt. His fight was quiet, but it was far from over. He belonged in that restaurant as much as anyone, and as long as he remained, he would do more than survive—he would endure.

The summer heat seemed to press down on Nonu as he pushed open the back door of the bustling restaurant for the last time. His heart pounded with a mix of anxiety and exhilaration. He had spent two years in that kitchen, slaving over the stove, enduring the scalds and burns, and facing the endless litany of orders barked out with little regard for his humanity. Today, he had taken a stand. Today, he had chosen himself over the job.

Nonu strode out into the alley, the acrid smell of garbage mixing with the tantalizing scent of spices still clinging to his clothes. He glanced back at the familiar sight of the kitchen, its heat shimmering through the glass window, the cooks moving in frenzied patterns, all part of a dance he had known too well. But now, it was a dance he was stepping away from.

He recalled the endless hours, the thankless tasks, and the relentless pressure from his boss, Andre. Andre had always been on his case, pushing him harder, demanding more, never a word of praise or recognition. Just this morning, as Nonu was slicing tomatoes for the lunch rush, Andre had stormed over, berating him for not working fast enough. The tirade had lasted barely a minute, but it had been the final straw.

In that moment, as Andre's words scalded as sharply as boiling water, Nonu had felt something snap inside him. He had murmured, "I quit," barely audible over the clamor of the kitchen, but the silence that followed spoke volumes. The other cooks had stopped, knives mid-air, all movement ceased for a fraction of a second as they absorbed the shock of his declaration. Then everything resumed as if nothing had happened, but for Nonu, everything had changed.

He walked further down the alley, his steps echoing off the brick walls, the midday sun casting long shadows. Nonu's mind whirled with possibilities and uncertainties. What would he do now? He had no concrete plans, only a dormant dream that now had the space to grow. He imagined traveling, exploring new cuisines, flavors, and techniques. Maybe even opening his own small venue someday, where he could cook with passion and authenticity, free from the oppressive demands of bosses like Andre De Jengo.

As he emerged onto the bustling street, Nonu took a deep,

cleansing breath. The city was alive and chaotic, but he felt a newfound stillness and freedom within himself. The world was wide open, and for the first time in years, he felt like he was finally free to explore it on his own terms. It was terrifying, but it was exhilarating. Nonu smiled to himself, the first genuine smile in a long time, and set off to rediscover his love for life and cooking. In course of looking for new opportunities, Nonu got a taxi driving job. Nonu was now on the street where he discovered more of the America's problems, he had been earlier informed about.

On his first day of driving, Nonu turned the key in the ignition, and the taxi's engine roared to life. He took a deep breath, glancing at the rearview mirror to ensure his rented cab was in pristine order. The streets awaited him, teeming with the untold stories of countless lives. Each day brought a new chapter in his book of experiences, but the burden of America's problems weighed heavily on his shoulders.

As Nonu navigated through the bustling streets of New York, he couldn't help but notice a young woman huddled on the sidewalk, her face etched with despair. He drove past her, but her image lingered in his mind. It was just one of many scenes that painted a bleak picture of the city he had come to know so well. Every corner seemed to tell a story of struggle—homelessness, addiction, inequality. It was a far cry from the American Dream he had once envisioned.

His first passenger of the day was a middle-aged man in a faded suit, the creases on his forehead deep with worry. As the man slumped into the back seat, Nonu sensed a heavy air of resignation. They exchanged polite greetings, and Nonu began to drive towards the specified address. The silence in the cab felt loaded, the man's eyes glued to his phone, probably seeking some solace in his digital world.

"Long day at work?" Nonu ventured, hoping to lift the man's spirits.

The man sighed. "Long year, if I'm being honest. This economy... lay-offs, you know? Just trying to keep my head above water."

Nonu nodded, understanding all too well. His previous job at the restaurant had been a casualty of the same merciless tide. He recalled the sense of helplessness, the gut-wrenching moment when he had to walk away from the only source of stability he had known in this foreign land. He drove on, a silent companion to the man's woes.

As the day progressed, Nonu encountered an eclectic mix of humanity. There were tourists with wide eyes and open wallets, blissfully unaware of the city's undercurrents. There were the night shift workers, shuffling in exhausted and grateful for a seat, even if only for a short ride. And then there were the families—mothers juggling groceries and children, fathers with weary expressions, trying to make ends meet in a world that seemed to care little for their efforts.

Each ride gave Nonu a glimpse into lives entwined with struggle and resilience. He became an unintentional confidant, a witness to the everyday battles fought by ordinary people. Through rain-soaked evenings and sunlit mornings, he drove on, absorbing the essence of a nation grappling with its own identity.

One night, he picked up a woman in her early twenties, her face partially obscured by a hoodie. As she climbed into the back seat, Nonu noticed her trembling hands. She directed him to a shelter on the outskirts of the city, and as they drove, a story began to unfold—a story of abuse, escape, and the quest for safety.

"Is it always this hard?" she whispered; her voice barely audibles over the hum of the engine.

Nonu's heart ached. "Sometimes it feels that way," he said softly. "But every day you keep going, that's a victory."

The woman nodded, her eyes glistening with unshed tears. She was a living testament to the quiet strength that lay at the heart of America's streets—a strength often overshadowed by its struggles.

As the city lights flickered by, Nonu realized that his taxi had become more than just a source of income. It was a lens into the soul of a nation. The roads he traveled were paved with stories of both despair and hope, and each passenger added a new layer to his understanding of America's complexities. He drove on into the night, the weight of these shared burdens a constant companion, but also a reminder of the unyielding spirit that kept him, and his passengers, moving forward.

One day, he picked up a black and white couple in his taxi. The female was a white woman, and they were supposed to be going to where the female's mother lives. On arriving there, the female asked her man to wait in the taxi, and that her mother said the dog in the house doesn't like black people. The man and Nonu all glanced at each other and later burst into long laughter, asking how does the dog know who is black and who is white?

As Nonu turned off the engine, an uneasy silence settled over the cab. The man in the backseat shifted uncomfortably, his laughter fading into a look of resigned irritation. Sensing the tension, Nonu cleared his throat, attempting to dissolve the moment's awkwardness.

"People say the darndest things, don't they?" Nonu said, trying to bring a lighthearted twist to the heavy atmosphere. The man didn't respond immediately, instead looking out the window and taking in the picturesque suburban neighborhood, where manicured lawns and white picket fences starkly contrasted the undercurrent of discrimination.

After a pause, the man finally spoke, his voice weary but measured. "It's not the first time I've heard something like that. It's funny, but not in the ha-ha kind of way, you know?" His eyes met Nonu's in the rearview mirror.

Nonu nodded, understanding more deeply than he let on. "Yeah, people sometimes don't realize the impact of their words. They think it's just a harmless joke, but it carries a lot more weight."

The man leaned forward slightly, arms resting on the back of the passenger seat. "You ever have those moments, Nonu, where you realize there are parts of the world that just haven't changed as much as we'd like to think?"

Nonu chuckled softly. "Every day. This job lets me see the city in ways I never did before. I get to hear people's stories and sometimes their prejudices. Makes the world seem a lot smaller and bigger at the same time."

The man smiled ruefully. "I hear you. It's like everyone has these invisible lines they draw, and they're all afraid to cross them. Even a dog's caught in the middle now."

Before Nonu could respond, the woman returned to the cab, a tense smile plastered on her face. She looked first at her partner and then at Nonu. "Sorry about that, guys. My mom...well, she has some outdated ideas. We should probably go."

As they pulled away from the curb, the atmosphere inside the cab was thicker than before, the man's earlier laughter replaced by an unsettling quiet. Trying to move past the awkwardness, the woman attempted to change the subject.

"So, Nonu, how long have you been driving a taxi?" she asked, her voice strained but polite.

"Just a few months," Nonu replied. "It's interesting work. You meet all kinds of people."

The man, seeking solace in connection, leaned in. "Any memorable stories?"

Nonu thought for a moment, carefully navigating the conversational minefield. "Oh, a few. There was this one time I picked up a writer who was researching a book on the different neighborhoods of the city. He had some fascinating insights into how places change over time, how communities evolve."

The woman tried to engage. Her earlier discomfort still evident. "That sounds interesting. Did he talk about this area at all?"

Nonu nodded. "He mentioned it. Said it's a place where people are trying to hold onto the past while pretending, they're all about the future. It can be... well, complicated."

The man sighed, looking at his hands. "That's one way to put it."

They drove on in silence for a few more minutes, the weight of unspoken thoughts pressing down on them. Finally, the man spoke again, his voice softer.

"You know, if a dog can be trained to sense people's discomfort, maybe we can learn something from that. Maybe it's about time we unlearn those invisible lines we've drawn."

The woman squeezed his hand, tears welling up in her eyes. "I'm sorry, Jim. I... I didn't think it would be like this. I thought... I thought we could just be ourselves."

Nonu glanced back, his expression one of quiet empathy. "Sometimes," he said, "the world doesn't make it easy to just be. But that doesn't mean we stop trying."

They drove on, the silence in the cab now a shared space of reflection rather than discomfort. Nonu pulled over at their destination, and the couple stepped out, exchanging a meaningful look before the woman leaned back into the cab.

"Thanks, Nonu," she said softly. "For everything."

Jim nodded in agreement. "Yeah, thanks. Maybe this world's a bit better with people like you in it."

As Nonu watched them walk away, he smiled to himself, starting the engine once more. The streets ahead were the same, but today's journey had cast them in a new light. He couldn't change the world in a day, but he could drive a bit of understanding through its veins, one ride at a time.

He pulled back into traffic, ready for the next fare, carrying with him the hope that maybe, someday, the story would be different. As Nonu was about to take

his mind off the previous encounter, and get to business, he got a call from someone he least thought of calling him. "Hello!" "Who is this?" "Hey Nos, this is me your friend from home." The person on the other end of the line said. "My friend from home?" Nonu wondered. "Yes. Your friend, Dee." The caller introduced himself. "What?" "Dee Nann, from Hill Land?" Nonu asked in surprise. "Yes, yes," Dee affirmed it, then laughter ensued. "What...?" "Wow!" "Where are you calling from?" Nonu asked, eagerly. "I am calling from Des Moines, Iowa." "What?" "Where is that?" "When did you get there and how did you?" Curiously, Nonu asked. "Long stories, my friend. long stories. Des Moines is here in America" Dee said with unhidden excitement. "So, you mean you're in America now? Well, I'm working right now, I'll call you back tonight when I get home." Nonu, ready to get back to work, promised Dee. "Okay, call me. I'll be waiting. Bye!" Dee said and hung up.

Later that night, Nonu got home and settled for a while before calling his friend back. Nonu leaned back in his chair, the phone still warm from the call with his friend. The request to move to another city was unexpected, but it wasn't what disturbed Nonu the most. It was the revelation about Raphael and the aftermath of his death that hung heavily in Nonu's mind.

"Accidentally killed his uncle all in the name of traveling to America," Nonu murmured to himself. He had always known his friend to be responsible and careful. How could something like this happen? The details were sparse during the call, overwhelmed by sobs and the weight of guilt in his friend's voice. Yet, the impact of those words was clear, and they echoed relentlessly in Nonu's thoughts.

Raphael was more than just an uncle; he was a mentor and benefactor. He believed in his nephew's potential, but even he didn't support his dreams of moving to the U.S. To have that life tragically cut short by the very person he helped was a cruel twist of fate. Nonu could almost see Raphael's face—kind, encouraging, always full of life. Nonu remembered the last time he saw Raphael on the refugee camp. Raphael had left the camp after diplomats from Benin told the Ogoni crowd that America has problems. The thought of that life being extinguished so abruptly sent a shiver down his spine.

Then came the details of the funeral. Nonu wondered how his friend managed to stand through it, knowing he was the cause of everyone's mourning. The image of a small, somber gathering flashed before him—black-clad figures, red eyes from crying, the air thick with grief and unanswered prayers. He imagined his friend standing apart, drowning in guilt and sorrow, unable to meet anyone's eyes. Depression had engulfed his friend completely. The lively conversations and laughter they once shared felt like memories from a different lifetime. The vibrant energy and optimism were now replaced with an unbearable heaviness. Nonu understood despair, but this was something deeper, more corrosive.

Moving to his friend's city was a monumental decision. Nonu knew it would be a tremendous upheaval, but could he really refuse someone in such a state of distress? The thought lingered as he weighed his options. Deep down, he felt a pull towards the person who needed him the most right now. *"I need to be there for him,"* Nonu resolved silently. The commitment felt daunting, yet necessary. He would need to navigate his own life changes, but he couldn't abandon his friend. Not now, when he was needed the most. As Nonu began to formulate a plan, a sense of purpose started to replace his initial shock. This was going to be difficult, but he knew one thing for certain: he would move mountains if it meant helping his friend find his way back from the darkness.

CHAPTER 20

NONU RELOCATED

Nonu's friend, Dee Nann, is from Hill Land, a community in Ogoniland. It was the only community in Ogoni where the people refused to join in the struggle for environmental justice. Not that Hill Land community was free from environmental degradation, but politics and government appointments were more important to the leaders than what affects the entire Ogoni nation. For this, they refused to get involved. Even when Dee's uncle, Raphael Nann, got to the refugee camp, it didn't take long when he left. As soon as he heard of the America's problems and that there was going to be very few people who will gain resettlement, he picked up his bag and left for home. Dee's uncle was the one who advised Dee not to go to the refugee camp when it was still active. But Dee's big dream was always about going to America, and that dream did not die.

As kids in Hill Land, you must not dream of what you cannot afford or achieve. And if you dare mention a thing above your level, you are seen as a bad child. So, when Dee Nann, 19, told his mother and siblings that he would travel abroad, particularly America, where he would attend college and study to become somebody, his mother and siblings all berated him for having such giant ambitions without any money available to embark on a journey of such magnitude. Dee's mother and siblings do not even know him as one with big dreams. But there he was. Dee believes in the philosophy of dream big and leave the rest for God to handle. Not quite a month after Dee made that declaration to his mother and siblings, something big happened. The community erupted in a life-changing event. An Oil Company operating in Hill Land community would pay for damage done to farmlands that would positively impact lives in the community.

In Hill Land, life is a mixture of good and evil. As an industrial small town sprawling every year, all kinds of activities go on. Originally, it was a sleepy town of 80 thousand, but due to its industrial nature, Hill Land had grown to a million people living in it. There's a harbor where shipping industries line up the coast. Oil companies actively operating scattered across the land. Oil workers spend cash for the women who need them. Despite the wealth in the land, Dee grew up a poor boy. Dee's father died when he was 5-year-old. Raising him and five other children by his mother was tough. But Mrs. Nann worked hard. Because Dee had experienced poverty, he wanted anything and everything humanly possible that would erase generational poverty from the family and provide good life for his mom and siblings. But the thing though, neither his mother nor siblings knew the contents of Dee's mind. So, when he told them he would travel abroad, they almost condemned him. "What? What did you just say?" Dee's mother screamed. Continuing, Dee's mother said. "If you think I will sell any piece of land that we don't have for you to travel abroad, you're joking." "Your father did not have this type of high ambition. From where did you get this?

Maggie Nann, Dee's mother questioned. But Dee was not fazed by whatever his mother had said.

A month later, news of oil spill compensation began spreading around the town. And if everything should go accordingly, the family of Nann should receive about 3 million U.S. dollars in compensation due to damage to the family vast farmland by oil companies operating there. When Dee Nann heard the news, he could hardly believe his ears. His uncle's words echoed in his mind, over and over, each repetition bringing a fresh wave of disbelief and elation. Three million dollars. The amount seemed almost impossible to comprehend. The family's long-standing farmland, their ancestral home, had been a source of stability, but also of hardship. The last few seasons had been brutal: droughts, pests, spillage, and financial pressure had worn them down. That all would change with a single piece of news: a recompense for the damage inflicted by large corporations—a windfall no one had ever expected, was impossible to believe. But it was the truth.

"I told you mom. I told you I was going to travel." Dee said excitedly. His mother's joyful sobs filled the room, but Dee's thoughts were already thousands of miles away, soaring across the ocean to the land of his dreams. America. The word itself was like a ticket to possibility, a plane soaring through his imagination with endless destinations. Dee had pictured this moment countless times, visualizing skyscrapers reaching into the sky, streets filled with vibrant energy, universities bustling with knowledge, and people from all corners of the globe converging in one melting pot of culture and ambition.

He sprinted to his room, his heart racing. Years of hopes and dreams scribbled in his worn-out journal suddenly felt tangible. He flipped through its pages, where he had meticulously researched American cities, universities, scholarships, and opportunities. Los Angeles, New York, Chicago. It was all there—the potential pathways his future could take. To him, America was not merely a geographical location; it was a symbol of limitless dreams, a canvas where he could paint his aspirations now turned experiences within reach.

Dee sat at his desk, staring at a map of the United States pinned to the wall. Every pin and mark on the map pulsed with new significance. He ran his fingers over the Atlantic Ocean, tracing a path from his small village halfway across the world to the East Coast of America. His future did not seem distant anymore; it vibrated with the vivid reality of an impending adventure. This compensation would turn his fantastical   daydreams into practicable plans. He envisioned himself blending into the fast-paced flow of Times Square, standing at the base of the Statue of Liberty, and walking the halls of a renowned American university.

The rest of the day passed in a blur of excitement and planning. Dee could hardly stay still, his mind racing with possibilities. He sat down with his parents, discussing what this windfall meant for all of them. His uncle's voice, infused with a mixture of pride and relief, outlined potential investments and improvements for the family's future. Yet his mother's eyes sparkled whenever the conversation turned to Dee's dreams. She had always berated him for aiming high, often reminding him that the world does not end in America. "There are other opportunities out here if one dared to reach for them." Madam Nann would tell her ambitious son.

Letters and brochures from various American universities piled up on his desk, collected over the years through tireless inquiries and applications. Dee spread them out, each one a portal to a possible future. Harvard. MIT Stanford. Drake University. Institutions that had previously seemed like distant stars now felt like places he could genuinely aspire to join. The funding was no longer a haunting query; the hurdle had been removed.

Dinner that evening was a celebration. The entire family gathered, and the atmosphere was electric. Dee's siblings, younger in age but equally enthusiastic, peppered him with questions about life in America. "What's the first thing you'll do?" one asked. "Will you go see the Grand Canyon?" asked another. Dee laughed, their excitement reflecting his own.

"To study," he replied, his voice firm with resolve. "I want to learn as much as I can, bring that knowledge back, and make a difference here." His words drew applause and cheers, but internally, he was filled with a mix of determination and thrill. To learn, to grow, to experience everything the world had to offer—that was his mission.

As the night deepened, Dee slipped outside, needing a moment alone to absorb the magnitude of what lay ahead. The stars in the clear night sky felt closer somehow, as if they too were celebrating his impending journey. He inhaled the cool night air, filled with the scents of home—earthy, familiar, grounding. It was bittersweet, the thought of leaving, but it was overwhelmingly overshadowed by the potential that awaited him.

Staring up at the stars, Dee whispered to himself, "America, here I come." His heart swelled with gratitude, excitement, and unshakable resolve. The dream was no longer a distant hope; it was a breathtaking, imminent reality.

It's been two weeks since the news of 3 million dollars compensation was coming to Dee's family. Excitement and celebration had overwhelmed Dee. The money finally came, signaling his traveling to America was real. But something happened. One of his 3 uncles had stepped up effort to convince Dee not to travel to America, telling him "America has problems." Dee's excitement and happiness was now turning into sadness and frustration. But Dee has not given up yet. He continued to follow up with his application with Drake University in Des Moines, Iowa.

Dee sat on the edge of his bed, staring at the worn-out ceiling. His room, usually filled with vibrant colors and thick air of hope, now seemed cloaked in a dull, oppressive gray. The long-awaited 3 million dollars had finally arrived, a beacon of hope and a promise of dreams realized. Traveling to America had been his ultimate goal for as long as he could remember, a dream nurtured and cultivated through years of hard work and resilience. Yet, the joy that initially overwhelmed him was now subdued by an unexpected hurdle – his uncle's relentless efforts to strip away his confidence. Just two weeks ago, the atmosphere in Dee's home was electrifying. The news of the compensation had spread like wildfire, igniting celebrations among family and friends. Dee had danced with his sisters, laughed with his brothers, and shared hearty conversations with his parents about the wondrous possibilities that awaited him in America. He visualized himself walking through the bustling streets of New York City, attending classes at a prestigious university, and building a prosperous life. The taste of his long-desired future was almost tangible.

But then his father's younger brother, Raphael, surfaced from a corner of the extended family tree with a dark cloud of negativity. Dee had always regarded Raphael with a mix of admiration and wariness. Raphael was older, seemingly wiser, and always opinionated. He, too, had wanted to travel outside of his country. That was why he went to the refugee camp that he couldn't follow through. However, he had never taken a keen interest in Dee's life until now. The sudden surge in Raphael's concern was baffling. Raphael began by dropping casual remarks about America's crime rate, expensive healthcare, and political unrest. Initially, Dee brushed off these comments as ignorance or mere jealousy. But as days passed, Raphael's words grew more persistent and insidious.

"America has problems, Dee. Why waste your perfectly good life over there?" Raphael's voice echoed in Dee's mind, casting shadows of doubt over his dreams. "They don't care about us immigrants. You'll just be another face in the crowd, struggling and suffering." Raphael would insist.

Dee's hands clenched into fists, his nails digging into his palms as he fought to maintain composure. It was infuriating how Raphael's words began to gnaw away at his initial unwavering excitement. He had always been certain of his decision, driven by the aspiration to carve out a better life and broaden his horizons. How could a few comments sow such seeds of uncertainty?

His family's reaction didn't help either. His mother, though supportive, began to voice her anxieties, no doubt fueled by Raphael's incessant warnings. "What if he's right, Dee?" She whispered one evening, her eyes filled with worry. "The world is unpredictable. We just want you to be safe."

Dee's heart ached as he saw the fear etched on his mother's face. He longed to offer her a sense of comfort, but the mounting pressure was suffocating. The confidence that had once surged through him now felt like a fragile thread.

Walking down the streets of his hometown, Dee noticed how familiar paths and faces began to blur into a background of melancholia. The place he had always known now felt simultaneously comforting and confining. His best friend, Aman, tried to lift his spirits. "Didi!" Aman called out. "Don't let Raphael get into your head. You've worked hard for this. America has its challenges, but it also has countless opportunities. This is your dream, man. Don't let anyone take it away from you." Aman consoled.

Aman's words sparked a flicker of warmth, but the emotional tug-of-war within him was relentless. Every time he closed his eyes, Dee was torn between vivid visions of his bright future in America and the shadowy doubts planted by Raphael.

Every evening, alone in his room, Dee would sit and write in his journal. He poured out his emotions, hoping the act of writing would help dispel his fears. "Why now?" he scribbled angrily on one page. "Why try to break me when I'm so close?" The journal became a battleground for his conflicting emotions. On one page, he would outline his plans and aspirations, detailing the universities he dreamed of attending, the courses he was eager to enroll in, the places he yearned to explore. On the next page, he would list the warnings and concerns, each one gnawing at his resolve. As the days passed, Dee realized that the battle he faced was not just external but deeply internal. It was a test of his faith in himself and his dreams. He understood that Raphael's attempts to dissuade him came from a place of fear and possibly love, but it was up to him to decide the path he would take.

One night, Dee took a deep breath and planned. He would not let Raphael's fears become his own. The journey ahead might be fraught with challenges, but it was his journey to make. Dee closed his journal, feeling a newfound sense of determination. The road to America was no longer just a dream but a goal he would fiercely pursue. He owed it to himself and to the unyielding spirit that had brought him this far.

The first one week of Nonu's time with his friend Dee, he had his ears full of stories upon stories. He was dumbfounded to hear everything his friend had told him. But he was willing to hear more. Nonu's friend's apartment is a cozy and welcoming space. Upon entering, you are greeted by a small foyer that leads into a spacious living room. The living room is filled with natural light, thanks to the large windows that offer a view of the city skyline. Comfortable couches and armchairs are arranged around a coffee table, making it an inviting place to relax. The walls are adorned with art pieces and photographs, giving it a personalized touch.

The kitchen is modern and well-equipped, compared to Nonu's apartment when he first arrived. Stainless steel appliances and a sleek island that doubles as a breakfast bar reflects a modern accommodation. Adjacent to the kitchen is a dining area with a wooden table and chairs, perfect for small gatherings or dinner parties. Living there, Nonu felt a strong sense of comfort and contentment. The apartment's warm decor and friendly energy make it feel like a home away from home. Nonu particularly enjoyed the quiet evenings spent in the living room, reading a book or having deep conversations with his friend.

CHAPTER 21

DEADLY ENCOUNTER

In Dee's family, what was thought to be mere lovely concerns suddenly took a 90-degree negative turn. Dee's uncle's opposition to his nephew's traveling abroad ambition developed into something else. Intensifying his opposition against Dee's idea of going to America, Raphael brought his close friend to convince Dee to drop the idea of traveling to America. As soon as Raphael's friend opened his mouth to speak, Dee was able to notice the jalouse undertone quickly.

"Dee, you know you don't have to spend all this time and money that your family don't have just to go to the United States." Jim, 50, spoke through his mustard filled mouth. "My son, Tenee, he's older than you, he didn't travel abroad, but he's graduated in Agric. Science. I'd advise - you have a second thought and find a way to seek admission into one of the universities here at home, that would surely be better for you than wasting all this money on traveling to the U.S. That place has a lot of problems. Get it?" Feeling very upset, Dee stood up from his seat to walk out of their sight, but his uncle, Raphael, stopped him. *In an attempt to free himself, Dee hit his uncle in the throat, killing him instantly.*

Dee stared blankly out of the small, dust-smudged window of his room, his heart heavy with an unimaginable burden. The late afternoon sun cast long shadows across the worn floorboards, but Dee's eyes saw nothing but the haunting memories of that fateful moment. He had replayed the scene a thousand times in his mind - the heated argument, the desperation, and finally, the unthinkable accident that took Raphael's life. Each replay tore at his soul, deepening the chasm of grief and guilt that threatened to swallow him whole.

The family home, once a place of boisterous joy and familial warmth, now felt like a mausoleum. Silence hung in the air, heavy and oppressive, punctuated only by the occasional muffled sobs that came from Raphael's wife, Dee's mother, and Aunt Lila. Raphael's aged mother had taken to sitting in his old room, surrounded by his belongings, as if by some miracle, he might walk through the door once more. Her eyes, red-rimmed and hollow, bore the look of someone who had seen the world crumble before her and was left holding the irreparable pieces.

Dee's mother and siblings, usually the pillars of strength and wisdom in the family, were shadows of their former selves. His mother, Maggie, moved through the house like a ghost, her once lively chatter replaced by a haunting silence. She could barely look at Dee, her eyes reflecting a mix of sorrow and confusion. How could her beloved son, the one she had so carefully nurtured and protected, be the cause of such tragedy? Dee's 2nd uncle, Lakae, had retreated into himself, spending long hours in the garage under the pretext of work, but everyone knew he was simply looking for an escape from the unbearable present.

The pain within the household was palpable, an entity unto itself, feeding off the broken spirits of those within. Conversations, once lively and filled with laughter, were now forced, stilted, and rare. Meals were somber affairs, with the clatter of cutlery against plates sounding like thunder in the suffocating quiet. Dee could barely bring himself to eat, knowing that each bite was flavored with the bitterness of guilt and regret.

Dee's siblings, who had once looked up to him with admiration, now regarded him with a mixture of fear and bewilderment. They avoided his gaze, their young minds unable to comprehend how the brother they had idolized could be involved in such a terrible incident. Dee longed to reach out to them, to explain, to beg for their forgiveness, but words seemed inadequate. What could he possibly say that would bridge the chasm that had yawned open between them? Every effort felt like a failure before it even began.

The community, too, was not untouched by the calamity that had befallen Dee's family. Neighbors who had once waved and chatted warmly now passed by with furtive glances and hushed whispers. There were sympathetic looks, sure, but also those of judgment - a collective grappling with the understanding that someone they knew was capable of such an act. Dee felt their eyes on him, a constant reminder that his sin was not only personal but public as well.

In the depths of night, when the house was at its quietest, Dee often found himself in Raphael's room. He would sit on the edge of the bed, running his hands over the bedspread, now covered with layers of memories. The room still smelled faintly of Raphael - a mix of his favorite cologne and a hint of the leather-bound books he loved to read. It was here that Dee allowed himself to weep, to release the torrent of emotion that he kept bottled up during the day. His tears wet the pillow, his sobs shaking his frail frame as he whispered apologies into the void. "I'm so sorry, Uncle Raphael. I'm so sorry." "I didn't mean to do this to you, uncle." "Please, please, forgive me, for-give-me, uncle." Dee wept profusely, asking forgiveness from his late uncle.

Raphael's dreams had been just as vivid, just as urgent, as Dee's. The reason why he even joined the refugee movement in the first place. Only he couldn't make it. And when Raphael returned, he became closer to Dee than ever before. They had spent hours together, talking about the future, about the possibilities that awaited them beyond their small town. Yet, Raphael had always been skeptical of Dee's plan to move to America, warning him of the potential pitfalls and the heartache of leaving behind their roots. Their final argument had been a reflection of all the tensions that had simmered beneath the surface - the clash of dreams and reality, the weight of responsibility versus the call of adventure. And in one horrific moment, it had all crumbled, leaving nothing but loss and sorrow in its wake. Dee's life, once filled with the aspiration of a better tomorrow, now felt like a prison of yesterday's mistakes. The dream of going to America had lost all its luster, replaced by the grim reality of the present. It was no longer a goal but a ghost, haunting every waking moment, a stark reminder that some aspirations come with a price too heavy to bear.

As days turned into weeks, the wound in the family's heart remained raw and bleeding. Would they ever find a way to heal, to forgive, to move forward? Dee didn't know. All he could do was navigate each moment, hoping that time, in its relentless march, would somehow bring a modicum of peace to the shattered remains of his family and melt away what had been a deadly encounter.

CHAPTER 22

THE FUNERALS

"**W**ow!" Nonu expressed shock listening to his friend's account of the deadly encounter between Dee and his uncle back at Hill Land, Ogoni in Nigeria. Nonu was able to gather himself up and ask about how the funerals went. And Dee kept pouring it out like water gushing out of a funnel.

"Under a somber, overcast sky, the tight-knit community gathered at the modest home where the planning for Raphael's funeral began. I, still shattered by the dreadful accident, sat pale and silent in a corner, eyes fixed on the floor. The living room, thick with the scent of lilies and murmured condolences, hosted Raphael's immediate family and close friends, all grappling in quiet dismay with the task at hand." Dee narrated; his face paled as it could be. But he continued.

Mrs. Eliza, Raphael's wife, took the lead, her grief-stricken face creased with resolve. "Let's ensure that Raphael gets a service befitting the wonderful person he was," she said, her voice wavering yet determined. Through tears and shared memories, decisions began to take shape. "His favorite hymn, 'Amazing Grace,' must be played," suggested Mrs. Eliza, her hands trembling as she scribbled notes. Several heads nodded in agreement. Raphael had a penchant for simplicity, a life lived without unnecessary pomp, and so they decided the service would reflect his nature—modest yet profoundly heartfelt.

Next came the question of location. The family church, St. Michael's, a place where Raphael had spent many Sundays in quiet reflection, seemed the fitting choice. Its stone walls and stained-glass windows felt like a comforting embrace to those who had grown up under its roof. They debated over details—flowers, music, eulogies—each choice a small tribute to the man they had lost. Raphael's brother, Thomas, insisted on delivering the main eulogy, determined to convey the essence of the brother he'd adored since childhood. Tuka, a close friend, volunteered to sing at the service, her voice carrying the poignant sorrow of someone who had lost more than a friend.

By the time the planning concluded, dusk had fallen. The living room, now cleared of scattered papers and takeaway coffee cups, felt heavy with the day's emotional toll. As the family departed to gather what rest they could before the ceremony, Dee lingered, trying to find words to express the depth of his regret. But no words came, only silence and a promise to honor Raphael's memory to the best of his ability.

The morning of the burial arrived with an unexpected surge of sunshine, casting a serene glow across the churchyard as the casket was carried inside. The air, thick with the fragrance of blooming roses and freshly turned earth, seemed to whisper a reluctant farewell. Inside St. Michael's, mourners assembled in reverent silence. Candlelight flickered along the walls, casting gentle shadows over the rows of pews where friends and family sat, clutching tissues and programs alike. Mrs. Eliza, clutching a handkerchief embroidered with Raphael's initials, led the procession, her steps heavy with loverly sorrow.

The service commenced with the hymns Raphael so loved. Tuka's voice soared, filling the space with a bittersweet melody that brought many to tears. When Thomas took the podium for the eulogy, his voice strong despite the tremors of grief, he painted a vivid picture of Raphael's life—his generosity, his laughter, the small, unforgettable acts of kindness that defined him. Though the words brought tears, they also brought smiles, fleeting but genuine, as memories surfaced of Raphael's antics and unwavering support. The shared sorrow turned, momentarily, into a celebration of a life well-lived, albeit cut tragically short.

"As the service concluded and the congregation rose to pay their last respects," Dee explained. "I approached the casket, my steps slow and deliberate. Kneeling beside it, I suddenly whispered an apology, one last chance to seek forgiveness I feared I might never achieve. The sorrow in my heart merged with the lingering scents of incense and flowers, a heavy reminder of the cost of a single, irrevocable moment that was as deadly as it could be." Dee said, pausing for a fresh breath, then continued.

Finally, the pallbearers, their faces set in determined solemnity, lifted the casket and carried it through the arched doorway, sunlight reflecting off its polished surface. Outside, under the expanse of a crystal blue sky, Raphael was laid to rest beside the old oak tree in the churchyard—a place of peace he would have cherished. As the final shovelful of earth settled over the grave, the community lingered, sharing hushed conversations and distant stares. For them, today was not just a farewell but a covenant to remember and honor Raphael in the smallest of gestures, the quietest moments. As they began to disperse, the sense of loss remained, intertwined with the memory of a man who had touched each of their lives indelibly.

CHAPTER 23

BENEATH THE GUILT

Dee Nann sat by the window of his almost delipidated room, the dim light casting elongated shadows on the worn wooden floor. His eyes followed the path of raindrops racing each other down the glass, merging into larger rivulets, mimicking the tears he no longer had the strength to shed. Raphael's burial had drained him, leaving behind an ache that gnawed at his insides, heavy as a millstone. A month had passed, but grief still clung to him like a second skin. Guilt, a relentless adversary, whispered in his ear, questioning every action, every decision he had made. Was it the right thing to swing his hand at Raphael just to free himself? Was Raphael right at all to invade his decision to travel abroad? Dee was in absolute disarray about what exactly happened on that fateful afternoon.

Late one night, after hours of restless pacing, Dee pulled out the crumpled letter Raphael had left. Its edges were frayed from constant unfolding and refolding, the ink smudged where tears had fallen. The words, a mix of encouragement and finality, pushed Dee to reclaim his abandoned plans. America beckoned, an escape route and a battlefield for his torment. Heavy with purpose, he decided it was time to leave.

The next few weeks were a blur of bureaucracy and silent suffering. Dee found himself frequenting sterile government offices, a stark contrast to the chaos swirling inside his mind. First, he needed a passport, but his old one had expired, the corners of its cover curling from disuse. He filled out forms with robotic precision, his mind elsewhere while his pen scrawled answers to mundane questions. The clerk, a woman with a sympathetic smile and tired eyes, processed his application with the efficiency of someone long accustomed to the mechanical routine.

Next, Dee sat for the mandatory photograph, the flash blinding him momentarily. His reflection, captured in the split-second burst of light, looked hollow, the smile a mere tick he had forced his face to adopt. Days turned into weeks as he waited, each passing moment adding to the weight he carried. The call finally came, his passport ready to be picked up. He accepted it with a nod of gratitude, clutching the small booklet as if it were his lifeline palpable.

Next came the visa, a hurdle Dee wasn't entirely sure he could clear. The embassy was a fortress of glass and steel, intimidating in its modernity. Long lines of hopeful applicants snaked through the lobby with their collective palpable anxiety. Dee filled out another set of forms, a mirror of those he had already completed for his passport. The interview, scheduled days in advance, loomed ominously. Dee stood before the embassy, a beacon of glass and steel that seemed to reach towards the sky. Its formidable presence sent shivers down his spine and stirred a mix of apprehension and determination within him. As he entered, he couldn't help but feel dwarfed by the long lines of fellow applicants, each one carrying a heavy burden of anxiety.

Clutching his carefully filled-out forms, Dee couldn't help but notice the mirroring of his own journey. The passport application, a gateway to new possibilities, now eerily resembled the visa forms he had to complete. Each question he answered was a reminder of the meticulous process he had already undergone.

Days of anticipation led up to the scheduled interview, an encounter that held the key to his dreams. It loomed before him ominously, casting shadows of doubt upon his hopes. Doubts about his worthiness, his preparedness, and whether he would be able to convince the authorities of his intentions.

But amidst the fear that threatened to consume him, Dee held onto a flicker of hope. It was the same hope that had driven him to pursue this path in the first place, the same hope that had pushed him to overcome countless obstacles along the way. He reminded himself of the passion burning within him, the burning desire to explore, to learn, and to grow.

As Dee approached the interview room, he took a deep breath, trying to steady his racing heart. He reminded himself that this was not the end of his journey, but rather an important chapter in the larger narrative of his life. The outcome of this interview would certainly shape his future, but it would not define him.

With each step towards the door, Dee mustered the courage to face the unknown. He knew that he had done everything in his power to prepare, and that he had poured his entire being into these aspirations. Whatever the outcome, he promised himself that he would keep pushing forward, navigating the twists and turns of this unpredictable journey.

As Dee entered the interview room, he reminded himself of his worth and the depths of his determination. He would face this challenge head-on, armed with his resilience and unwavering belief in his dreams. The visa may be a hurdle, but Dee was ready to leap, ready to soar towards the life that awaited him on the other side.

On the morning of the interview, Dee dressed in his best suit, the one he had worn to Raphael's burial. The fabric still carried the faint scent of lilies, mingled with the sting of formaldehyde. The scent clung to him as he made his way to the embassy, a macabre reminder of the past month's events. He waited his turn, heart pounding like a war drum, each beat echoing the doubts that refused to be silenced. Finally, his name was called. Dee stepped into the interview room, where a stern-faced officer sat behind a desk. The interrogation began, a barrage of questions designed to peel away any deceit. Dee answered them all, his voice steady despite the turmoil inside. When asked about his purpose, he spoke of education that would eventually lead to new opportunities, of forging a new path in the land of dreams. To backup his purpose, Dee presented an admission letter sent to him from Drake University in the city of Des Moines, Iowa, U.S.A. The officer, satisfied with his responses, stamped his papers with a curt nod. With his visa approved, Dee felt a slight lift in the weight he bore. It was not a relief, not yet, but a semblance of progress. The final task was booking the flight, a straightforward process he completed online. As the departure date approached, his emotions oscillated between trepidation and resolve.

The day of his departure arrived, overcast yet calm. He packed his suitcase methodically, each item placed with care, as if order in his luggage could translate to order in his life. Dee's departure was a whirlwind of emotions for the entire family. Preparations for his journey began weeks in advance, with his mother, Maggie, taking the lead. She meticulously curated a list of essentials, ensuring Dee had everything he needed for his new adventure. Each evening, after dinner, the family would gather around the dining table to check off items from the list. His younger siblings, Leera and TorBari were enthusiastic helpers, albeit in their own unique ways. Asira, ever the practical one, took Dee shopping for clothes suitable for the colder climate he would soon encounter. She taught him how to layer his clothes properly, fretting over the quality of the thermals and the fit of the woolen socks. As they shopped, she shared old stories of her friends who had moved abroad, painting a picture of challenge and opportunity.

On the morning of his departure, the house buzzed with a mixture of excitement and sorrow. Leera made sure Dee's favorite breakfast was ready, her little hands struggling to balance trays filled with parathas and chai. Dee's family are attuned to some Indian cuisines and always shopped for them. The aroma of spices was intermingled with the heavy scent of impending farewell.

The drive to the airport was filled with intermittent bursts of conversation and prolonged silences. Asira sat next to Dee, her hand occasionally finding his, offering a squeeze of reassurance. TorBari and Leera sat in the back, their moods oscillating between sadness and pride for their big brother. Dee arrived at the airport hours early, the throng of travelers, a comforting anonymity. He moved through security, the monotony of procedure a distraction. Sitting at the gate, he stared at the boarding pass in his hands, the printed details blurring as memories of Raphael washed over him. But beneath the sorrow and guilt, a sliver of hope glittered, fragile as gossamer.

Leera, with her innate curiosity, peppered Dee with questions about his upcoming life: "Will you have a monkey as a pet there?" she asked one evening, her eyes wide with innocent wonder. SorBari, quieter but equally devoted, would sneak little notes into Dee's suitcase, hoping they would offer comfort in moments of homesickness. He carefully folded a hand-drawn map of their neighborhood, labeling each street and house, so Dee would always remember home.

At the airport, time seemed to speed up. Security checks and baggage drops blurred together, but amidst the rush, Asira hugged Dee tight, whispering prayers and blessings into his ear. Tears shimmered in her eyes, but her voice remained steady, filled with the strength she hoped to impart to him. Leera clung to his leg, her small frame shaking with sobs, while SorBari stood a little apart, fighting hard to keep his emotions in check. He handed Nonu an envelope, saying, "Open it when you miss us."

As Dee walked towards the departure gate, he turned back one last time. There they stood: his mother, the anchor of his heart, waving frantically with both hands; and with a brave but trembling smile. Dee felt a surge of love and gratitude, knowing that no matter how far he traveled, the bond with his family would remain unbreakable. With a final wave, he stepped into the unknown, carrying with him the spirit of home. All happened beneath the guilt.

CHAPTER 24

DEE TRAVELS

Dee entered the airplane, a totally new experience. He had not travelled by flight before. He ran his eyes all around the flight. He touched, felt, and smelt it before finally taking his seat. As Dee boarded the plane, he felt the full weight of his journey. Raphael's absence loomed large, but within the tight confines of the aircraft, a new beginning awaited. Dee took his seat and fastened his seatbelt, the engine's hum resonating through his bones, a prelude to the journey ahead. With a deep breath, he closed his eyes, ready to face whatever the future held, carrying his past not as a burden, but as a testament to his resolve.

Sitting at seat number 51, his assigned seat, Dee looked out the airplane window, memories of what transpired between him and his uncle, Raphael, in his parents' living room washed over him. He remembered the back-and-forth argument with Raphael over his decision to travel abroad. More so, the last one that resulted to the death of Raphael. Dee wished Raphael had reasoned with him, and concluded if he had, what happened would not have happened.

Raphael had always wanted to become a teacher, but he never got the chance. Dee's dream of traveling to the U.S. was confused with being stubborn between them, and Dee promised to live fully in honor of his uncle's unfulfilled aspirations.

Their bond had been more than just familial; it was a brotherhood solidified through years of shared laughter, secret handshakes, and endless discussions about their future. Dee recalled one evening when he was about ten years old. He had snuck out after dinner to join his uncle at their favorite spot by the river. Laying on the soft earth, they stared at the stars.

"Wouldn't it be amazing, Dee," Raphael had said, "if we could travel to places where the stars look different? Imagine seeing the sky from another part of the world!" Dee had agreed enthusiastically, although at the time, the idea seemed improbable – more a child's fantasy than a future. Dee didn't know any better then and was only following the lead of a senior uncle. So, Dee always agreed to whatever Raphael had to say. But as they grew older, Raphael's ambitions turned inward. He set his sights on improving their village, bringing education and hope to the younger generations. Meanwhile, Dee's longing for the broader world never faded but was tempered by a sense of guilt. "Was it right to leave when there was so much to be done at home?" Dee would occasionally ask himself.

The emotional storm inside him continued to rage, even as Dee found himself succeeding in school and acquiring skills that could take him abroad. He worked tirelessly, balancing studies and part-time jobs, fueled by a determination to transcend the limitations of his environment. He would often find solace in Raphael's unwavering support. On particularly hard days, Raphael's words echoed in his mind: "You're going to make it, Dee. For both of us." But Raphael was mistaken that to mean at home, he never thought Dee's dream was abroad.

After Raphael's passing, the village felt colder, lonelier. Dee threw himself into preparations for his journey, not just for himself but out of a deep sense of duty to prove to his uncle he was capable. The days before his departure were a blur of logistics, goodbyes, and moments of doubt.

Yet, sitting on the plane, feeling the vibration of the engines as it taxied down the runway, Dee's resolve crystallized. He was not running away; he was carrying Raphael's spirit with him. The dreams they shared belonged to both, and Dee understood it was now his role to live them out.

He tightened his grip on the armrest as the plane lifted. He could almost hear Raphael's voice amidst the hum of the engine: "I forgive you, Dee. I forgive you. I'll always love you. And be with you everywhere you go. Your success is mine. It's all of us' success." Dee closed his eyes, feeling the surge of the plane as it climbed into the sky. Despite the sadness, there was also a seed of excitement growing within him. This journey was a beginning, not an end. It was the first step of many, a testament to the enduring bond between him and Raphael. And as the plane broke through the clouds, the sun's rays bursting into view, Dee vowed to embrace every moment, every challenge, and every opportunity the future held.

He had not left his uncle behind; Raphael was with him, a guiding light in every decision he would make along the way. Dee opened his eyes to a world of possibilities, the promise of adventure laid out before him like an uncharted map, ready to be explored. Then the plane touched down at JFK International Airport in New York City from where Dee would board another flight to Des Moines, Iowa, his destination.

CHAPTER 25

THE TWO BONDING BODIES

6:00 AM Saturday Morning -- At 6:00 am on a Saturday morning, the world awakens to a serene, almost magical atmosphere. The sky, a canvas of delicate pastel colors, shifts seamlessly from shades of deep indigo to soft pinks and oranges, heralding the arrival of the sun. The first rays of sunlight stretch lazily across the horizon, casting a golden glow that bathes everything in a warm, gentle light. So does Nonu, who wakes up feeling very light and gentle having been pent up for months with emotions, stress, and anger ever since he moved in with his friend, Dee. Whistling, Nonu prepares coffee well enough for more than two people. As the coffee brewed, Nonu took a stroll to the balcony.

On the balcony Nonu could feel the air. Crispy and invigorating, it carries the subtle scent of dew-kissed grass and blooming flowers. Every breath feels fresh, a reminder of the purity and promise of a new day. The stillness of the early hour is punctuated by the gentle rustling of leaves as a mild, refreshing breeze glides through the trees, making them sway gracefully. The neighborhood is tranquil, with only the soft cooing of morning doves and the occasional chirp of early birds breaking the silence. The birds' morning songs, filled with joy and enthusiasm, create a harmonious symphony that complements the serenity of the moment. Nonu stood and watched houses, silhouetted against the soft light, stand quietly, their windows catching the first glimmers of the sun's rays. Gardens glisten with droplets of dew, each blade of grass and petal sparkling like tiny diamonds in the nascent sunlight. A few early risers can be seen, quietly stepping out for a morning jog or watering their plants, exchanging silent nods of greeting with others who cherish this peaceful time of day. Nonu was carried away but the sound of the coffee maker in the house signaling the coffee brewing was over made him get back inside the house.

"Hey Dee!" "You drink coffee?" Nonu called out as he filled his cup and his friend's. "Yes, man!" "Okay, I got you." Nonu said, assuring Dee he was filling for him as well. Shortly, they grabbed their cup of coffee and headed to the balcony again. The distant hum of a waking city begins to subtly fill the background, a reminder that soon the world will fully come to life. But for now, this perfect morning holds a timeless quality, a brief, precious moment where peace and beauty reign supreme. The day ahead holds promise and potential, but the tranquility of this early hour is a gentle reminder to savor the quiet and the simple joys of life.

Out on the balcony, the two had friendly conversations. "I didn't sleep much last night." Nonu started. "Why?" Dee asked. "I was just going over all that happened between you and your uncle back home. I think your uncle was right. America really has problems. And Mr. Randolph, the Benin man who told the Ogoni people in the refugee camp that America had problems was also right." Nonu said those words with straight face. "I mean, real talk." He added. Dee couldn't response. It was like he's been tormented. "I'm not trying to rub whatever that happened on your face, but I'm just letting you know that my experience here in the States informs that those guys were right. You get me?" Nonu concluded. "Sure, sure." Dee said. "I'm not going to talk about it now. I'm trying to grow out of it and focus on my school. However, I appreciate the fact that you're being sincere, and I thank you for that, you know?" Dee said and stretched out his hand to Nonu for a handshake. The two shook hands and sipped their coffee. Nonu took another sip and cleared his throat. Then, he said: "But I'd say one thing though. I am very grateful to the Heroes of the Ogoni Struggle. I am humbled by those Invisible Victims of our noble struggle. The reason is that without them, I wouldn't know the America's problems." Sure, you're right on that, man". Dee said in response. "Because of them I'm studying journalism in a prestigious University today." Dee nodded in agreement with what Nonu said.

Nonu and Dee's friendship blossomed in the layback city of Des Moines. Their serendipitous encounter from and in the U.S. quickly turned into a bond that neither had anticipated. Nonu's journalistic curiosity often meant that he asked deep, insightful questions, which Dee found refreshing. Dee, with his passion for the environment and his dream of becoming an environmental lawyer, found in Nonu a patient listener and sometime participant in his causes. Their shared background from Ogoni, a place known for its historic struggles and rich cultural tapestry, provided a unique bond that few others could understand. Sitting on the balcony of their apartment, overlooking the city skyline, they often found themselves discussing their beloved

Ogoni land. Nonu would often recount tales of Ken Saro-Wiwa, how his words had inspired him to pursue journalism. Dee, on the other hand, often worried about the environmental degradation back home. "If only we could make a difference," Dee would muse, his eyes reflecting a determination that Nonu admired deeply.

Despite their academic pressures, they made time for each other. They attended community events, rallied for environmental causes, and even participated in cultural festivals. Their college experience in the U.S. was a blend of learning and activism. Both of them faced their own battles. Nonu, as a refugee, found it challenging to adapt initially. The trauma of displacement haunted him, yet Dee's presence provided solace. Dee's own past was marred with guilt, a shadow that he carried from the tragic incident involving his uncle. Living with Nonu, however, began a healing process for him.

Their evenings were often filled with debates and discussions. The news of environmental disasters would spark fervent debates - Dee bringing in the scientific facts, while Nonu brought in the human stories. They complemented each other's strengths. Nonu's storytelling abilities added a human touch to Dee's data-driven arguments. Together, they started writing articles for their college newspaper, highlighting issues from their homeland and relating them to global environmental concerns. Their unique perspectives made them popular among their peers and professors alike.

The fall season, with its tapestry of crimson and gold leaves, casts a magical spell over school campuses across countries in the western hemisphere. Students, bundled in cozy sweaters, eagerly anticipate the beginning of the fall semester. The crisp air invigorates their spirits, making walks to classes a delightful experience. The scent of pumpkin spice wafts from the campus café, and study sessions are often held under the canopy of colorful trees. There's an unspoken camaraderie as students share stories of summer adventures and look forward to football games, homecoming events, and the promise of new academic challenges. Fall is a time of renewal and anticipation, a season that perfectly mirrors the academic journey. Yet, for Nonu, it was the semester that he had difficult decision to make either to continue or drop out of school.

Fall semester of 2009, Nonu enrolled in the Literature of the Third World class in the English Department at his school. Invigorated as other students, Nonu was ready to learn as his Journalism course required him to take the class. One morning, the class was in full session, and Professor Nancy Watkins was lecturing. Before any students could know what was going on, Nancy had derailed on her course. "What do you guys think of when the African Americans say black is beautiful?" This question had no bearing to what the day's lecture was about. And for that, students were reluctant to response. One could not actually tell if Professor Nancy felt frustrated by students not giving her the response she expected. "What if we say they should go back to their boat?" Nancy spewed.

As the words tumbled from Professor Nancy's lips, an eerie silence enveloped the classroom. Nonu's heart skipped a beat, his grip tightening around his pen until his knuckles turned white. He had enrolled in Drake University with a heart full of hope, looking for a safe haven where minds were open, and education meant enlightenment. Instead, he found himself grappling with the same ugly specter of racism that haunted his nightly taxi shifts.

For a moment, no one moved. The students, a diverse mosaic of backgrounds and experiences, exchanged bewildered glances. Dee could see the shock mirrored in their eyes, like ripples spreading through a still pond. A young African American woman sitting at the front, whom Dee had come to recognize as Alisha, seemed to withdraw into herself. The confident, vibrant persona she usually displayed in class was momentarily eclipsed by a look of deep hurt.

Nonu's mind raced. He thought about the young man he had driven last night, a promising lawyer who confided about the subtle racism he faced daily. He recalled the elderly woman who reminisced about marching in the civil rights movements, only to see her grandchildren fighting the same battles. And here they were, in the supposed sanctuary of academia, faced with a stark reminder that ignorance was not confined by walls.

Alisha finally broke the silence. "Professor, I have to say I'm deeply offended by your comment," she said, her voice shaking yet resolute. "To suggest that African Americans should 'go back to their boat' ignores centuries of history, pain, and triumph. This is our home as much as anyone else's." Another student, a white young man named Luke who often participated in class discussions, added, "I agree with Alisha. That kind of rhetoric is dangerous and divisive. It's disappointing to hear it from someone we look up to for knowledge."

Professor Nancy seemed taken aback by the backlash. She opened her mouth to speak but hesitated. Nonu could see a flicker of defensiveness cross her face, followed by a forced calmness. "My intention was not to offend," she said, a weak attempt at damage control. "I was merely provoking a discussion on the complexities of racial identity." But the damage was done. Nonu felt a tangibly different energy in the room—a collective pullback from an unspoken line that had been crossed. His own experiences of racism and exclusion now felt amplified, each past slight echoing louder in his memory.

"I think what we need," said a soft, yet stern voice from the back, belonging to Maya, an immigrant student from India, "is to understand why such phrases like 'Black is beautiful' exist and the history of oppression that makes them necessary. Instead of questioning their place in this world, we should be questioning the systems that necessitate such affirmations."

The room murmured in agreement. Nonu was proud of his classmates for standing up, yet profoundly disappointed that they had to do so in the first place. These were supposed to be the spaces where minds expanded, not where old prejudices were reinforced. Trying to collect himself, Nonu spoke up. "I came here believing this was a place where we could break free from the societal chains that bind us, explore ideas, and foster inclusivity. Comments like that pull us back into the darkness we are trying to emerge from." Professor Nancy shifted uncomfortably. "I see I've upset many of you. It was not my intention, and for that, I apologize."

Nonu felt a semblance of relief, but it was drowned by a lingering unease. An apology might soften the blow, but it couldn't erase it. He knew the taste of such moments—a bitter mix of progress tainted with regress; hope laced with disillusionment. The class eventually moved on, but the atmosphere was irrevocably altered. By the end, students filed out more somberly than usual, their minds heavier with the reality that even the halls of education were not immune to the prejudices that plagued the rest of the world.

Nonu made his way to the door, pausing to look back at the now almost-empty room. Alisha and a few others were still deeply engaged in a private conversation. Maya gave him a nod as she passed, a silent solidarity in her eyes. AS Nonu walked home from campus, he couldn't help but indulge himself in deep thinking. Anger filled his heart, to say the least.

Nonu arrived home. Dee was inside but Nonu didn't say a word to him. Nonu walked straight to his room and pushed the door close. Concerned about the sudden strange behavior, Dee tapped on Nonu's door. "Hey Nos, are you okay? What's up with you?" Curiously, Dee asked, pushing the door open. Lying face down on his bed, Nonu faintly said a few words and informed Dee he might not be attending the lecture on reparations scheduled for the evening on that day. "No, you will go. We are going." Dee said. Dee continued to persuade Nonu not to feel bugged down by what Nancy had said. "You know the African slaves did not just get their boats and sail to America. Your professor knew that too. She's only being ignorant. Oh, you think because she's a professor she can't be ignorant?" "Come on man, we are attending that lecture tonight." Dee said, chuckling. "Okay then. Let me take a rest." Nonu said and dozed off.

The evening came and was time for the public speaking event inside the 775-seat Sheslow Auditorium at Drake University. The speaker from Canada, a female, was to speak on "Making the Case for Reparations." By her opinion, the African Americans are not the right recipients of reparations, if there should be such things. According to her, the home countries of Africa should be the proper place to direct a reparations payment to. She made mentions of how she met Moshood Abiola on a flight sometime in the past and they had a discussion on the issue. Abiola was from Nigeria and was the champion of reparations for slavery, but unfortunately, he died in prison. The millionaire contested in the 1993 presidential election – the very election the Ogoni people boycott – but the army Gen.

at the time arrested him after Abiola declared himself the winner. He later died in prison.

When the woman was done speaking and was time to take questions, Nonu raised up his hand. He was recognized and microphone passed on to him. Nonu's heart pounded in his chest as he stood among the murmuring audience, gripping the microphone tightly. The lecture hall was abuzz with tension and curiosity, the air thick with the weight of the recent address. He cleared his throat, locking eyes with the Canadian speaker who had just delivered a contentious viewpoint on reparations.

"If I may," Nonu started, his voice steady but impassioned, "is it proper for the Ogoni people and Ken Saro-Wiwa to demand reparations for the damage done to their land by Shell Oil?" The woman paused, her poised expression softening slightly. "Absolutely," she replied. "It is entirely proper. The Ogoni people's plight and the environmental devastation wrought by Shell Oil is a grave injustice. Ken Saro-Wiwa was a courageous activist who paid the ultimate price for standing up against corporate and governmental oppression. It is tragic that Nigeria executed Saro-Wiwa and others in their fight for justice. Reparations in such a context are not just proper—they are necessary."

A collective murmur of approval and reflection spread through the audience. Nonu could see heads nodding, students and faculty members absorbing the implications of her acknowledgment. He felt a sense of relief at her validation, but also a pang of sorrow remembering the sacrifices of Ken Saro-Wiwa and the enduring struggles of the Ogoni people.

Another hand shot up from the back of the room. It was Maya, the same student who had stood against Professor Nancy's ignorant remark just days before. "Considering your stance on reparations for the Ogoni people," she began, "how do you reconcile that with your position that reparations should not be paid to African Americans here?"

The speaker sighed deeply, gathering her thoughts. "My argument is based on the idea of direct harm and accountability," she explained. "In cases like the Ogoni, there›s a clear party responsible for specific actions and damages. However, the African American situation, while undoubtedly deserving of justice and equality, is more complex due to the historical nature of slavery and systemic racism—that's where direct reparations become contentious. I believe we should target systemic change and economic equality measures."

Dee, sitting next to Nonu, felt a surge of frustration, whispered in Nonu's ear before raising his hand up. When the microphone was passed on to him, he asked: "But isn't systemic change and reparative justice interconnected? Can we truly fix systemic racism without acknowledging and compensating for the damages done? African Americans have been systematically excluded from wealth and opportunities for generations. Doesn't that deserve reparative action?"

The audience buzzed with agreement, and Dee saw the determination in their eyes. The speaker nodded thoughtfully, taking in his words. "You raise an important point, Dee," she said. "It's crucial that we address the systems that perpetuate inequality. Perhaps a combination of direct reparations and systemic reform is needed to truly heal these deep wounds." A faculty member, Professor Williams, who specialized in African Studies, weighed in. "Canada has its own history with First Nations peoples, where direct reparations and systemic reforms are both being pursued. Can we not draw parallels to understand how reparations for African Americans could also encompass both elements?"

The hall filled with a new sense of purpose, students eagerly engaging in the debate, their voices rising together in a chorus of shared commitment to justice. Dee took a deep breath, feeling a glimmer of hope. This conversation was more than just about reparations; it was about creating a world where every voice could contribute to a narrative of equality and rectification. As the session concluded, Nonu and Dee felt a newfound resolve. Both approached the speaker afterward. Dee, extending his hand. "Thank you for addressing my question. These discussions are so vital." She shook his hand warmly. "And thank you for challenging me, Dee. You guys' perspectives are invaluable."

7:30am the following day, Dee and Nonu headed out for their morning lectures. When they arrived on campus, Dee took the track that leads to his building while Nonu proceeded to Merideth building that housed the School of Journalism and Mass Communication. Abruptly, Nonu stood frozen at the entrance to the building, his eyes locked on the harsh scribbles. The note, with its jagged edges and angry letters, seemed to scream from the door: "We will not welcome a water war on this campus." His heart thudded heavily in his chest, each beat reverberating with a mixture of anger, fear, and bewilderment.

Bitter thoughts swirled in his mind. The conversation from the previous evening replayed in his head, now tinged with a painful irony. He had believed in the power of discourse, convinced that raising important issues and confronting history's shadows through dialogue could pave the way for understanding and change. But this note revealed a stark reality—a jarring reminder of the deep-seated resistance to uncomfortable truths. "What does this even mean, a 'water war'?" Nonu thought, his mind racing. It was clear that whoever wrote the note had twisted his question about the Ogoni people and Ken Saro-Wiwa into something threatening, something they felt didn't belong on this campus. It stung that his attempt to bring a human rights issue to light, to seek empathy and justice, was met with hostility and intimidation. A wave of bitterness welled up within him. Nonu had come to Drake University searching for a place of learning, growth, and acceptance—a haven where justice could be pursued through education. Yet the note signaled a rejection of his very quest, an unwillingness to confront the uncomfortable parts of history that still reverberate today. It wasn't just an attack on him, but on the very principles of free inquiry and social justice.

With a heavy heart, Nonu headed toward his body Dee's class, ready to bring him to see the note on the entrance door. The weight of America's problems was now heavy on his shoulders and feared it shouldn't consume him. When Dee and Nonu arrived at the building entrance, he showed the note to Dee. Then, Nonu glanced around, wondering if anyone else had seen the note, if anyone else felt the same ripple of anxiety and hurt. Students passed by some glancing curiously at the note, others oblivious. Dee and Nonu felt isolated, as if the weight of the words and what they represented rested solely on their shoulders. Nonu's thoughts shifted to Ken Saro-Wiwa and the Ogoni people, how their fight had been met with violence and repression. Though a world away, their struggle felt intimately connected to this moment—another instance where speaking truth to power was met with backlash.

Taking a deep breath, Dee tore the note from the door. He crumpled it in his hand, feeling the rough paper dig into his skin.

This wasn't just about him; it was about refusing to let ignorance and fear dictate the narrative. He couldn't let this discourage him. It was a reminder, painful as it was, of why he needed to keep pushing, keep questioning, and keep speaking up.

He walked into the classroom; the note still crumpled in his hand. Eyes turned to him, a few sympathetic, others curious. Dee took his seat and spread the paper out on his desk, smoothing the creases. The act felt symbolic acknowledging the hatred and prejudice yet refusing to let it remain hidden or ignored. As the professor began the day's lesson, Dee's mind remained partly on the note and partly on his resolve. He thought about his classmates, the conversations they needed to have, and the change they could foster together. He thought about the bitter realities of systemic oppression, both in America and abroad, and the necessity of confronting them head-on, no matter how uncomfortable or unwelcome the truths might be.

Nonu skipped his morning class that day due to the offensive note on the entrance door to his class. At home in his bedroom, Nonu sat on his bed, staring at the television screen in disbelief. The news anchor's voice echoed in his mind: "Dee had been shot to death when walking home from school." A chill ran down his spine, and he felt a wave of nausea wash over him. Dee was more than just a friend; he was like a brother, someone who had always been there for him through thick and thin.

Memories of shared moments flooded Nonu's mind. He remembered the countless hours they spent playing cheeses, their late-night study sessions, and the times they confided in each other about their hopes and fears. Dee had a way of making even the darkest days seem brighter, and now, that light was extinguished forever.

Nonu's heart ached with a searing pain he had never felt before.

He wanted to scream, to break something, to cry out in agony, but all he could do was just sit there, paralyzed by grief. Questions swirled in his mind: "Why Dee? Why now? What kind of world is this where such senseless violence can take away someone so dear?" He felt a crushing sense of guilt, wondering if there was something he could have done to prevent this tragedy.

The house felt eerily silent, a stark contrast to the turmoil inside Nonu's heart. He glanced around the room, his eyes landing on a photograph of him and Dee laughing at a school event. Tears welled up in his eyes, and he clutched the photo tightly, as if holding onto it could somehow bring Dee back. Nonu's thoughts turned to the note he had seen earlier: "We will not welcome a water war on this campus." He wondered if it was connected to Dee's death, if there was more to the warning than he initially understood. His mind raced with possibilities, each one more disturbing than the last. He knew he couldn't stay silent. Dee deserved justice, and Nonu was determined to find out the truth behind his friend's death.

As the night wore on, Nonu lay in his bed, unable to sleep. The weight of his loss pressed down on him, suffocating him with its intensity. He vowed to honor Dee's memory, to be as strong and resilient as his friend had always been. But in that moment, all he could do was grieve, letting the tears fall freely as he mourned the loss of a brother taken too soon. "My bonding body is gone." Nonu shouted and kicked the coffee table Dee and him always sit, talk, laugh, and drink coffee.